I0717764

WITCH HUNTER

COVEN: BOOK 10

DAVID NETH

DN Publishing

Witch Hunter

Coven, Book 10

www.DavidNethBooks.com

ISBN: 978-1-945336-34-8
First Edition

Subscribe to the author's newsletter for updates and exclusive content:
DavidNethBooks.com/Newsletter

Follow the author at:
www.facebook.com/DavidNethBooks

Also by David Neth

<u>Coven</u>
Harpy
Siren
Valkyrie
Shapeshifter
Sorcerer
Witch (Short Story)
Enchantress
Oracle
Trickster
Poltergeist
Hex (Short Story)
Witch Hunter
Demon (Short Story)

<u>Under the Moon</u>
The Full Moon
The Harvest Moon
The Blood Moon
The Crescent Moon
The Blue Moon

The Art of Magic

<u>Fuse</u>
Origin
Omertá
Oblivion

<u>Heat</u>
Black Magnet
Dust Storm
The Gatekeeper

<u>Standalone</u>
All I Ever Wanted

CHAPTER 1

- DECEMBER 1989 -

It was the first time Samantha had been in the house across the street since they had defeated the shapeshifter. The house where she and her husband had been held captive. The house that sat directly across the street from theirs, as a constant reminder of everything that had happened just over a year ago.

To be sitting and sipping tea casually on some of the same furniture that had been in the house when they had been abducted was an irony that didn't slip her mind.

"Thanks again for having us over, Mr. Kors," she said to her neighbor. The new neighbors had moved in a little more than a year ago, not too long after the police had finished up their investigation.

"It's good that we finally got to do this," he said. "And call me

Gerald. We're neighbors, not colleagues." He reached in his pocket for his cigarettes and offered one to Steven.

Samantha's husband declined with a shake of his head, then motioned to his wife and said to Gerald, "Would you mind not smoking in front of Samantha? We don't want anything to hurt the baby."

"Huh?" Gerald studied them, then put the pack back in his chest pocket. "Oh. Oh, sure. How much longer do you have?"

"Hopefully not much." Samantha rubbed her belly. She was grateful for the cold weather and the fact that she could better hide her size under layers of sweaters. Not that she really needed them with the heat from the baby. "I'm due at the end of the month."

Pressing both hands against the arms of his chair, the old man swung forward once before rocking back and launching himself to his feet on the second try. He let out a groan as he stood straight. "That would be why Nancy was so insistent on inviting the two of you over. She wanted the both of you to enjoy a night before the baby came." He walked over to the credenza built into the wall. "You want a drink, Steven? To celebrate."

Steven cast a sidelong look at his wife before answering. "Um…sure."

Samantha knew that her husband was only accepting the drink because he had denied Gerald his cigarettes. For better or worse, her husband was a peacekeeper.

"What do you want? I've got scotch, whiskey, gin. You name

it, I can mix it."

"Um…whiskey, I guess."

Gerald smiled and reached for a glass bottle.

"Does Nancy need any help in the kitchen?" Samantha hated sitting and chitchatting while the elderly woman worked on the meal they were all about to enjoy. Judging by the savory scents wafting from around the corner, they were in for a treat.

"Nah, she's okay." Mr. Kors handed Steven a highball glass filled to the brim with the brown liquid. "If she needs something, she'll holler. She's already had me set the table real nice for you folks." He retook his seat and then raised it in the air in a toast. "To you two on this new parenting journey."

Steven obliged, raising his glass and then bringing it to his lips for a sip. Samantha covered her mouth as she watched, trying to hide the grin as she saw the displeasure clear on her husband's face. He wasn't much of a drinker, and when it did it certainly wasn't hard liquor.

The conversation fell into silence as Gerald enjoyed his drink. Steven took a few more sips and then set it on the table beside him.

Samantha looked around and admired the Christmas tree that sat in the front window. She had seen it from her house across the street, but it was more impressive in person. It shone bright with white lights and handmade ornaments made of paper, cardboard, and clay. She smiled, recognizing what exactly that meant. Someday she'd have a collection of crafts that her own child would make for her too.

"How do you like living here?" Steven asked.

"It's nice," Gerald said. "Quiet street. Nice neighbors. Even if it's an old house, it's not too bad. Keeps me young, going around and fixing everything that's wrong."

"Everything's beautiful." Samantha looked around at the garland hung around the cased doorways and the Christmas cards taped to the doorframe leading to the kitchen.

"To be honest, I think the previous owners did a lot of renovation work—well, two owners ago, I guess. The last ones were a bit—you know—loony."

Samantha looked down at her tea and smirked. She knew exactly how *loony* they had been.

"So how did that work?" Steven asked. "With the last owners, I mean."

"How did what work?"

"Well, they were…*killed*, right?"

Gerald nodded. "That's right."

"So how did you and your wife end up buying it?"

"Ah," the old man said with a nod and a smile. "You see, what happened here made a bit of a splash in the news—I can only imagine what you two thought, living just across the street. Maybe I should be asking *you* the questions."

Samantha hoped he wouldn't. She wasn't sure what lie she could come up with that would fit in with the story he had been told by the realtor who sold him the house.

"The house wasn't on the market long," Steven said.

Gerald shook his head. "No, it wasn't. But long enough for the realtor to start to get worried. See, she knew about the bodies they had found in the basement—and the blood up in the bedroom. She was eager to sell this place to get it off her caseload. And for the three weeks that it was listed, this place had no one coming to see it. Not a single person. From what I understand, the few people who were interested were turned away when they found out that several people had been murdered—and chopped up—in this place. So when Nancy and I saw it, we were able to negotiate a great deal."

"And the murders don't bother you?" Samantha asked.

He shrugged. "It's in the past. No murderers live here now. And the police brought a team in that cleaned everything up for us. This place was spotless when we bought it!"

"But isn't your master bedroom where one of the murders happened?" Steven asked. "The news said they found blood on the wallpaper."

Gerald made a face and shook his head. "Didn't like that wallpaper anyway. We ripped it out, put up new stuff that Nancy picked out. Some flowers or shit, I don't know. Don't care, either. I just sleep in there—and occasionally, other stuff."

Samantha raised her eyebrows at that comment and quickly thought of something to change the subject. "Well, you wouldn't be able to tell based on the way everything looks now. It's a very nice and inviting home."

Witch Hunter

Gerald smiled and opened his mouth to reply, but the front door creaked as it opened. Snowy, cold air hit them as a young man stepped into the house.

"Hey Dad," he said.

Gerald stared in surprise. "Dennis?"

CHAPTER 2

Bon Jovi blared from the speakers as Kathy leaned in close to hear her friend Trisha speak over the music.

"He's looking right at you!" Trisha tilted her chin to the guy across the bar who had been staring in Kathy's direction for the last ten minutes.

Kathy glanced back at him and smiled. He *was* cute.

"Don't tell me you haven't noticed him," Trisha said.

"Of course I've noticed him, but I still don't *know* him." The last thing Kathy wanted—or needed—was to get involved with someone. She was still a little nervous about even trying to date someone after she had completely made herself look like a freak with her last date, Jeff. And that's not to mention her on-again, off-again relationship with Jeremy, which was now definitely *off*.

She needed to be single for a little while.

At least until someone special came around.

"So go over there and *get* to know him!" Trisha said. "Take him upstairs for a private chat."

Kathy shook her head. "You know I'm not here for that."

"Isn't that why you moved out? To be able to do whatever you want? Your sister isn't here. Let yourself live a little!"

That was true. Kathy's apartment was just above the bar—and surprisingly looked very similar to the one she had experienced during her illusion at the hands of the trickster she and Samantha had faced back in May.

Kathy had been out on her own for about a month now and she had been playing it safe ever since, as if she were still under the watchful eye of her big sister. First her excuse was that she wanted to get settled into her new place. Then it was that she wanted to make sure her finances were in order before she let herself have any sort of fun that required spending money. And now it was…what?

"Look, the last few times we've gone out, you've had a problem with every single guy I've found for you," Trisha said. "How do you expect me to be a wingwoman when you won't even take my leads?"

She looked over at her friend and sighed, not that anyone could hear it over the noise of the bar. "Okay fine. I'll go ask him his name and see if he makes any moves after that. But if things get awkward—or weird—I'm out of there!"

"And I'll be here to help fend him off if need be. Just go and give this guy a chance!"

With butterflies in her belly—when was the last time she was nervous about talking to a guy?—Kathy slipped off the barstool and crossed the room. She only made it halfway before a different guy caught her eye.

Michael.

Jeremy's friend.

"Kathy?" he asked, wide-eyed with surprise.

"Hey!" Very naturally, they moved in for a hug that lasted longer than Kathy had expected. Not that she was complaining about that. She got along great with Michael, even if he had always just been Jeremy's friend to her. She hadn't seen him since May when she and Jeremy had broken up.

When they pulled apart, both of them smiled wide at each other, but neither knew what to say. Kathy *wanted* a conversation to suddenly spring up, but she couldn't think of a good enough thing to say to warrant that kind of discourse.

"How—"

"So—"

They both started talking and stopped when they realized they were about to talk over each other.

"Sorry," he said. "You go."

She shook her head. "No, it's okay. You can go." The best thing she could come up was to ask how he'd been. Small Talk 101. Lame.

"So Jeremy's been doing okay," he said.

"Yeah?" Her voice carried no interest, even though she *was* interested in how her ex was doing without her.

"Not great," he added. "Just okay."

"Is he still drinking?" She noted the irony. Asking the question while they stood in the middle of a bar; a few drinks already working their way into her bloodstream.

Michael pursed his lips and nodded. "Yeah, he is. Quite a bit. I'm actually moving out because things between me and him just aren't the same since college. I'm getting out of that party phase and he still seems locked in it. And I know it's only depression, but he refuses to even acknowledge it, which is so frustrating. Wow."

"What?"

"I sound like I'm his wife or something," he said with a chuckle.

She smiled, glad that he had successfully lightened the mood.

"I just don't want to watch him spiral anymore," Michael said. "And it's time I grew up and got my own place anyway."

"Well, I'm happy for you. Actually, I just moved out on my own last month."

His eyebrows raised. "You did? I didn't think you'd ever move out of that house!"

"With the baby coming soon and Samantha and Steven coming up on their first anniversary, I thought it was a good time to be on my own too." She pointed to the ceiling. "It's right upstairs."

"Is this your new hangout then?"

Her apartment—and the bar—were at the southeastern end of downtown, by the railroad tracks. Far away from the watering holes in Lawrence Park or the ones downtown that were often filled with college students from Gannon University—the crowds that she used to be drawn to not that long ago.

Kathy shrugged. "Guess so. I've only been here a handful of times, but I like it."

She looked past Michael and saw the guy she had been on her way to talk to. He was now nursing his drink, peeling the label off his bottle and no longer looking in her direction. She looked back at Trisha, who was deep in conversation with a man seated beside her at the bar.

"Looking for someone?" Michael asked.

She turned back to him. "Just checking on my friend. She seems to be occupied. Do you want to go upstairs so we could talk easier? This place is a little too noisy for me."

He smiled. "Sure. I'd love that."

CHAPTER 3

Nancy Kors emerged from the kitchen and her face immediately lit up, nearly as much as her Christmas tree.

"Dennis! What a surprise!" the woman shrieked as she wrapped her arms tightly around her son.

After his mother let him go, the newcomer moved on to hug Gerald. Samantha and Steven looked at each other, unsure of what to do. Samantha felt like they were suddenly crashing an intimate family moment.

"Come on in!" Nancy waved him forward. "Let me take your coat. Gerald, dear, take his bag!"

While she pulled Dennis's jacket off of him, her husband took the duffel bag out of his hands.

"What are you doing here?" Gerald asked. "I thought

you were at sea?"

"I was able to get an early leave." He turned to look at Samantha and Steven and asked, "I'm not interrupting anything, am I?"

Samantha put up her hand and shook her head with a polite smile. "Not at all."

"Don't worry about it," Steven added.

Gerald stepped back and stretched his arm out toward Samantha and Steven, who both rose. "I'd like you to meet our neighbors, the Harpers. This is Steven and his wife, Samantha."

Dennis shook both of their hands as polite pleasantries were exchanged.

"We were all just about to sit down to dinner," Nancy said. She looked to their guests. "You wouldn't mind if Dennis joined us, would you?"

"Mom, I don't want to impose or anything—"

"Really, it's no bother," Samantha said. "He's your son. Of course you want to see him. Maybe we should actually head home so you can—"

"No, you don't have to go and do that," Gerald said. "Sit! Stay a while! We can all get to know each other."

"It's just that Dennis is in the Navy and we don't get to see him very often." Nancy reached up and patted her son's cheek and beamed with delight.

"When the opportunity to come home early came up, I

knew I had to take it to surprise you guys as an early Christmas present," Dennis said.

Nancy wrapped her arm around his waist. "And what a wonderful surprise this is!" From the kitchen, the oven timer dinged. "Oh shoot. I need to go take the lasagna out of the oven. I'll be right back!"

After she disappeared into the kitchen, the room turned awkward again.

"Let's take a seat," Gerald suggested as he plopped back into his recliner.

Samantha and Steven both retook their seats while Dennis opted for the loveseat in the corner.

"So Dennis, you're in the Navy, huh?" Steven started.

"Yes, sir."

"I have a friend who's in the Navy. He was the best man at our wedding."

"What ship is he stationed on?"

"The *Constellation*?" Steven looked to Samantha for confirmation. She could only vaguely remember Robert mentioning what ship he was on. All she knew was that he was out in southern California now.

Dennis nodded with recognition. "Ah, so he's out of San Diego."

"Yeah, I think so."

"I'm on the *South Carolina*, out of Norfolk."

"How often are you actually out on the water?"

As Steven and Dennis continued their conversation, Gerald turned to Samantha and said, "I've noticed it was pretty dark across the street at your house. No lights again this year?"

She shook her head. "No. Christmas isn't really our thing."

"You had a wreath out last year. And some candles in the windows. Looked nice."

"That was my sister. She really loves the commercialism of Christmas, but she's out on her own now so the house is just mine and Steven's."

"So no lights?"

She shook her head. "Not this year, no."

"Are you Jewish?"

"No, I'm not," she said with a chuckle. Every time someone heard that she didn't celebrate Christmas, they immediately assumed that she was Jewish.

"So then what do you believe in?"

The question was brusque, but Samantha could tell he didn't mean anything by it. Still, it was an uncomfortable topic and one that she wished to brush off without any further question.

"Well, in December we sometimes celebrate the winter solstice."

Gerald narrowed his eyes. "What does that mean?"

"The shortest day of the year. The changing of seasons. It's more of a spiritual thing for us. Although, in the past, my sister has convinced me to get a tree and participate in *some* Christmas traditions. It's hard not to. I love gingerbread!"

The joke was her attempt to lighten the mood and shift the conversation away, but instead her words were noted by Dennis.

"You don't believe in God?"

Just as to-the-point as his father…

Samantha shifted in her seat. "Um…well…"

"My wife isn't a Christian," Steven said in her defense.

Dennis turned to Steven. "But you are?"

He shrugged. "It's how I was raised."

"And you're okay with throwing out your religion for her?"

"Just because we have some differences doesn't mean I can't respect what she believes," Steven countered.

Dennis shook his head. "I just don't see how that's going to work long-term."

"Uh…" Gerald cut in loudly, trying to diffuse the growing tension. "Samantha, are you going to do anymore Christmas traditions when the baby comes?"

She turned to her husband, again uncomfortable by the spotlight she was suddenly under. "Well, Steven and I haven't really discussed it yet…"

"Wait, you're having a *baby*?" Dennis asked, wide-eyed.

Nancy appeared in the doorway and cheerfully announced, "Dinner's ready!"

Relief washed over Samantha as they all rose and moved to the dining room.

Dinner was going to be hell.

CHAPTER 4

Kathy unlocked the door to her loft apartment and flicked on the lights. Michael walked in behind her.

"It's not much." She dropped her keys by the door. "I'm still in desperate need of furniture."

"But it's yours." He walked in and looked around.

In his presence, Kathy scrutinized her new living conditions. The whole apartment was a total of two rooms, the only private room being the bathroom, tucked in beside the kitchen. Two large windows opened up onto the street along one wall. Adjacent to that was a simple black and white kitchen with a short row of countertops, stove, and refrigerator, while a small bartop island contained the sink that overlooked the living room. At the wall closest to the door, there was a metal staircase leading up to the small loft area over the kitchen that served as Kathy's bedroom.

"It looks great," Michael added.

She stepped over to the kitchen as she chuckled. "It looks *cheap*."

"But, again, it's yours."

Shrugging, Kathy accepted his comment. "You want a drink?"

"You only have the bare minimum with furniture, but you have alcohol?" he asked with a laugh.

Holding up a bottle of vodka, she smiled, "You can tell where my priorities lie."

Just as she'd hoped, Michael laughed at her joke.

"No, most of my small stash here was a house-warming gift from Trisha," Kathy went on as she poured each of them their drinks. "Giving houseplants isn't really her style."

"Sounds like an interesting friend."

She walked around the island and handed him his drink. Together, they sat on the only couch in her living room area. It was a thirty dollar find from Salvation Army.

"Sorry for the lumpy couch," she said. "It was the best they had at the store and I was desperate."

"I don't think it's too bad." He winced as he adjusted his position.

"You want to know how I know you're lying?"

"Hmm?"

"I know for a fact that there's a loose spring in that cushion, so unless you like getting poked in the keister, you're just trying to be polite."

He smiled. "Okay, so you've got me."

Kathy took a sip of her drink to hide her own smile, which hadn't seemed to fade since he agreed to come up to her apartment. As much as she wanted to believe that it was pride in showing off her new place, she knew deep down that it was Michael that she was smiling about.

The room fell silent, with only the muffled sound of the bar downstairs rising up through the old floorboards. Kathy gazed off out the window and out of the corner of her eye she saw Michael staring at his drink.

Finally, she turned back to him and said, "So this is actually kind of awkward."

"Yeah. I just wish it wasn't."

"Are we being dumb? Trying to hang out without Jeremy? I mean, that's how we first met."

"No, I don't think so. We're friends, with or without Jeremy."

But he's the only reason we've ever spent any amount of time together, she thought to herself.

"I'm not sure I'm ready to see Jeremy—or talk about him, for that matter. The way we ended things…" She shook her head. "It was hard." Bringing the glass to her lips, she took a big gulp of her drink, feeling the alcohol kick in.

Easy there, Kathy, she thought to herself. *You've already had several downstairs. Pump the brakes before you end up spilling your guts about things you'd rather keep to yourself.*

"I understand," he said. "We don't have to talk about him— or what happened between you two. We can talk about other things."

"Like what?"

Michael took a gulp of his drink. "Um…well, how do you like living on your own? Is it weird not having your sister around as much?"

She took in a deep breath before responding. "Yeah, it's been an…adjustment, I guess you could say. It's like, when I was still living at home, when I was alone it was okay because I knew someone else would be home eventually. Now, when I'm home alone, I'm just…alone. It's weird. Nice at times, but also a really strange feeling."

"Well, if you're ever scared to be alone, you can always call me," he offered. "I'll be moving soon myself, but I'll make sure you have my updated number once I get it."

Kathy smiled as she circled her finger around her near-empty glass. "Thanks, but I can handle myself. Trust me."

"Oh, I know. You spent years putting up with…" He trailed off, not stating exactly who she knew he was talking about.

Jeremy.

"Yeah," she murmured.

"This is your first time living away from that big house on Arlington, isn't it?"

She appreciated the swift change in subject back to comfortable territory. "Yeah, I grew up in that house."

"Has your sister ever moved out?"

"Nope. She would stay at Steven's apartment before they were married, but only for a few nights. Really only when she was in college and claimed to be up all night studying with him, but I have my doubts about that. Then again, it's Samantha, so maybe she was *actually* studying all night."

Michael laughed. "She's pregnant now, right?"

"Yeah. Honestly, about to have the baby any day now. It was one of the reasons I decided it was time to get my own place. I can only be the third wheel in their marriage—their *family*—for so long."

"I'm sure she doesn't think of you as a third wheel."

Kathy chuckled. "You're right. She doesn't. But Steven certainly does. He's come around to me being a constant presence, but I get it. They need their space. And, honestly, so do I. I like having something that is one hundred percent mine. Well, as long as I pay the rent."

Michael laughed. "Yeah, that's kind of important."

"And a real downer," she joked. "Did you know bills come every month?"

Again, he laughed. "So I've heard."

"I hope it gets a little easier, though," she said, more serious. "This place is nice, and I know it's mine, but it still doesn't quite feel like home, you know? Whenever I think of home, I still think back to the house that I shared with my sister and the bedroom I had when I was a teenager."

"You have history with that old house," he said. "You'll develop history here too. It'll get easier. Trust me, from someone who has moved a couple times—including dorm rooms—each place feels like yours after a while. Less foreign."

"I know, I just…I can't get passed the fact that this place still smells faintly of paint, not that distinct family smell that comes from generations living in the same house."

He laughed again.

Is he flirting? Kathy wondered.

"You shouldn't be sniffing the paint. And besides, soon this apartment will smell of your distinct *odor* soon," he teased.

"Are you saying I smell?"

"In only the best way possible, of course."

"Oh, of course."

Definitely flirting, she decided.

"So what's Maddie been up to?" she asked, bringing up his girlfriend as a way to establish boundaries between them.

Michael studied his empty glass again. "Um…I'm not really sure what she's doing. We broke up."

"Oh, I'm sorry." Instinctively, she reached out and rubbed his shoulder.

"Yeah. Actually, it was shortly after you and Jeremy did."

"I'm sorry," she repeated. What else was she supposed to say?

"It's fine. You and I haven't really seen each other since you and Jeremy broke up, so you wouldn't have known."

"What happened?" she blurted before she could stop herself. Glancing down, she noticed her glass was empty. The alcohol was certainly beginning to loosen her lips. "If you don't mind me asking," she added.

"No, it's fine. Truth be told, it wasn't my choice, although I've come around to it by now. I mean, it's been more than six months, so I should be okay with it at this point, right?"

Kathy rubbed his back some more. "There's no timeline on how long it takes to get over someone. Especially when you were together as long as you and Maddie were. Three years? Four? That's a long time."

He nodded. "That's the thing, though. She wanted to settle down and get married and I'm…" He shrugged. "I don't know. I just wasn't there yet. At least, not with her. We had fun, you know? But to get married? Have kids? Maybe buy a house and spend our lives together?" He shook his head. "I wasn't sure if we had it in us."

"It sounds like you knew the end was coming, though."

"Yeah, that's helped me accept it."

"I know what you mean about not being ready to get married," she said. "It's like, I see Samantha and Steven and everything they have and I want that—I do. But right now? Not for me. I have a lot to settle about myself before anyone puts a ring on my finger or a baby in my belly."

"No, I agree—not that it's physically possible to put a baby in *my* belly," he joked.

"There's a trick," she added with a laugh.

They were quiet again. She kept her hand on his shoulder and he stared down at his empty glass again.

"You know," he started quietly, "when I saw you downstairs, I thought that it was a sign."

"Of what?"

"Well, you know. You're single, I'm single." He shrugged.

"Are you saying you and me?" She pulled away from him and made a face, but her smile ruined it. "Really? You think we'd be good together?"

"I don't know. Why not? Maybe."

She shrugged. "I guess it's not the *worst* idea."

They locked eyes and Kathy was suddenly very aware of how close they were sitting on the small couch. Of her hand on his shoulder. Of his leg brushing against hers.

Before she really knew what was happening, he was leaning in to kiss her, so she leaned in the rest of the way.

CHAPTER 5

Conversation had faded, leaving only the sound of cutlery on dishes as everyone silently ate their food. The tension from the living room had carried over during their meal and Samantha just wanted to get through dinner so they could make their quick exit without coming off as rude.

"Samantha, dear, you are glowing!" Nancy beamed from across the table as she cut into her chicken. She was obviously completely oblivious to the tension. "Pregnancy looks great on you."

Rubbing her belly, the witch smiled back politely. "It may look good on me, but it certainly doesn't *feel* good." She debated whether she wanted to start naming off the things on her body that ached or were tender or stiff, but she held off with Dennis's watchful eye from the other end of the table. As much as she wanted to believe he was just an inquisitive stranger, her gut was telling her not to list any weaknesses. "I'm just counting down the days."

"How much longer do you have?" Nancy asked.

"Two weeks."

"A Christmas baby?"

"Honey, don't." Gerald cautioned his wife with a slight shake of his head.

"What did I say?" Nancy asked, confused.

"The Harpers don't celebrate Christmas," Dennis said, his eyes locked on her. He clenched his silverware in his tight fists, like weapons.

"Oh." Nancy's smile faltered for a fraction of a second, before returning. "Well, that's okay. We all have our differences. What's important is that we respect one another."

"Exactly," Steven added.

Samantha shot her husband a look.

"So what are your plans for after the baby comes?" Nancy turned her attention back to her plate, unaware of the silent exchanges between her guests. "Taking care of a newborn is a lot of work. I know your sister just recently moved out. Gerald's semi-retired and I'm no longer working. We're right across the street if you ever need anyone."

"Thank you for the offer, but I think we'll be okay," Samantha said. "Kathy doesn't live too far, and she works right around the corner from here. I'm taking a couple months of maternity leave. The plan is to go back to work April first."

"And then what would you do with the baby?"

"Daycare, I guess." Samantha shrugged.

"We're worried about each step as they come," Steven clarified. "First let's handle the birth, then we'll worry about the childcare."

"I don't know about that," Gerald spoke up. "Our other son, Charlie, and his wife just had a baby last year. They were like you; thought they could handle daycare after the baby came." The old man shook his head. "There was a six month waiting list—and even then it cost a fortune. His wife ended up quitting her job because it didn't make sense to work just to pay for daycare."

Samantha could feel her pulse race as Gerald went on. The closer she got to her due date, the more she worried that she was forgetting something important or that they weren't truly prepared for a baby.

Steven reached over and put his hand on her arm to steady her. "I'm sure it'll all work out fine. If we have to, we'll rearrange our schedules until we can find daycare. By April, tax season will be winding down, so my workload will be letting up. And Samantha will miss it completely with her maternity leave. And I'm sure Kathy would love to help out too."

"April's right around Easter too," Dennis added. "Although I'm sure you don't celebrate that either."

"Dennis," Gerald warned. "Drop it."

"I just don't understand it. I mean, I'd get it if you were Jewish, but you said you celebrate the winter *solstice*? Who the hell does that? I mean, what do you believe in if it's not Christianity or Judaism?"

"There are plenty of other religions," Steven said in defense of his wife.

"Sure there are, but what group do *you* belong to? Or rather, which religion does Samantha believe in?"

"Dennis!" Nancy scorned. "You are making Samantha uncomfortable. She's simply an eccentric spirit. Let her celebrate whatever holiday she chooses."

"What exactly does that mean?" he pushed. "*An eccentric spirit.*"

"Leave it be," Gerald said firmly.

Dennis Kors set his silverware down on the plate in front of him. "I'm honestly curious. What do you mean when you say she's an eccentric spirit? I'm just trying to get to know your guests—your *neighbors*."

Samantha hated all of the talk about her as if she wasn't sitting in the room among the rest of them. But she still didn't speak up for herself because a part of her wondered exactly what the Kors would say in response to these questions.

"Your mother and I have lived here for just over a year," Gerald told his son. "We're hardly experts on what to make of our neighbors."

At least he's trying to back his way out of this conversation, Samantha thought to herself. *A neighbor who's only been here a year or someone who's spent their whole life living on this street, everyone has opinions about those who live around them.*

"First impression then," Dennis said.

Gerald sighed and looked first to Samantha, then to his wife. Finally, his eyes returned to his son before he spoke again. "In the short while that we've lived across the street from Samantha—and for most of that time, her sister as well—I have noticed some..." He rocked his head back and forth, then shrugged his shoulders. "...*oddities.*"

"Oddities?" Samantha blurted. "What kind of oddities?"

Nancy smiled at her. "I love how *different* you and your sister are. You march to the beat of your own drum."

"What does that mean?" Samantha pushed.

Steven put his hand on hers as a warning, but she ignored it and stared at her neighbors for an explanation.

"It's nothing bad," Gerald said, picking up on Samantha's tone. His face showed his concern for having upset her. "It's just that, last year when we first met when I went over to ask if I could borrow a rake because our yard was a mess with trees, I smelled...an odor coming from inside your house."

"An *odor?*" she asked.

"And this past winter, I could've sworn I saw you carrying a man into your house—and then I never saw him again."

Samantha swallowed down her worry. Her memory filled

with images of the oracle Oren, bleeding out on their couch.

"Strange men coming and going?" Dennis asked. "Who were these people?"

"Just one," Gerald said in Samantha's defense. He leaned closer to her. "I'm sorry for even bringing it up, it's just something that I've wondered about since I saw it. Who was that man?"

Samantha gave him a tight smile. "Oh, you know Kathy. She sometimes isn't too choosy about the men she brings home."

"But why were you carrying him into the house?" Dennis asked. "If it was a one-night-stand, then wouldn't he have been trailing behind your sister, ogling at her ass?"

"Dennis!" Nancy blurted.

"Who said it was a one-night-stand?" Samantha asked. Now she squeezed Steven's hand back to help give her strength to restrain her true comments.

"Isn't that what you implied?"

"Drunken friend," she corrected. "He needed a place to crash."

"Hmm," Dennis murmured, unconvinced.

The room fell silent as they all tried to recover from the barbs that had been traded. Samantha and Dennis studied each other from across the table, both of them hating the other, neither of them vocalizing it.

Steven made a point of picking up his silverware and cutting into the lasagna. "The food is good, Nancy!"

CHAPTER 6

Sun shining through the windows caused Kathy to stir. Before she had even opened her eyes, she reminded herself *again* that she still needed to pick up curtains for the windows. The morning sun always seemed to kill her plans to sleep in every Saturday and today was no exception.

Groaning, she rolled over and stretched, but stopped when she bumped into something. In a panic, she sat bolt-upright in bed and clutched the sheets to her chest.

There was someone in bed with her.

Looking down, she saw Michael's bare back. She only hoped that beneath the sheet, the rest of him wasn't bare as well.

"Oh my gosh!" she shouted as she tried desperately to recall the memories from the night before.

Her outburst stirred Michael and he rolled over and squinted his eyes. "Huh?" Realization hit him and he jumped to his feet. Or rather, he attempted to. The sheet got tangled in his legs and he collapsed onto the hardwood. When he stood, Kathy could see he only had his underwear on.

Immediately, she turned away to give him privacy as he scrambled for the other end of the sheet to cover himself up with. While he did that, she took an inventory of her own clothing. Pajama pants and an old T-shirt, just like always.

"What did we…?" Her voice trailed off, not wanting to bring herself to say the words—or to even think the thought.

Michael grabbed his jeans that had been draped over the banister at the edge of the loft and pulled them on. "I'm not sure." He hopped on one leg as he rushed to dress, struggling in his haste. "I remember you—*oomph!*—you offered to have me spend the night."

"I did not!" Kathy said defiantly. Her sister liked to tease her for her extensive dating history, but one thing Kathy was proud of was the fact that she hadn't slept with most of them. But to jump into bed with an old friend was new territory, even for her. She didn't want to deal with any of the implications that would follow that reality.

"Yes, you did," he insisted. "It's fuzzy for me too because those drinks were really spiked, but we were both yawning and talking about how it was getting late. I mentioned something about a cab and then you said calling a cab was a dumb idea because it was so expensive." He reached for his shirt and pulled it on before searching around the room for his socks.

Kathy warmed to Michael's version of last night's events. Money had been on her mind a lot since she'd been out on her own. It was one of the reasons she really only frequented the bar downstairs. At one point, she had added up how much she typically spent on a night out and she had been trying to forget that figure ever since. Worse, she cursed Samantha's accounting habits for rubbing off on her.

"I remember making a comment about sleeping on the lumpy couch," he went on. He had been successful in locating his socks and sat down on the bed to pull them on. "I don't remember exactly what you said to that. All I know is that somewhere along the line, someone suggested sharing the bed."

Kathy shook her head. "That must've been you who suggested that." But still, she wondered if it had been her. There was definitely some sort of sexual tension between them the night before. Had she invited him upstairs because she subconsciously hoped that they would end up in this situation? What did that mean for the way she felt about him? She had never really thought about Michael in that way before.

"Whoever it was that brought it up, I'm sorry for all of this." He fixed his pockets and backed toward the staircase. "I was really just going out last night for a drink. And then when I ran into you…" He took a deep breath. "It was just nice to see you, that's all."

She rose, following him toward the stairs. "There's nothing to apologize for. We're both adults. We can be civil, even after an awkward situation like this."

He smiled nervously and ruffled his hair. It was messy and flat from the pillow. "You're right."

Kathy looked over the banister into her small living room, locking eyes with the lumpy couch that supposedly put them in the bedroom to begin with. "Did you want to stay for breakfast or something?"

Michael met her eyes and smiled. "Actually, I'd like that. It'd help to have some food in me before I drive back to Lawrence Park."

"All right then." She started to descend the stairs. "I'll warn you, I'm not much of a cook. But eggs are so easy anyone can do them. And you can make the toast. I think I have some fruit in the fridge if—" She stopped at the bottom of the stairs and looked at him with her brow furrowed.

"What is it?"

"Didn't you kiss me last night?"

CHAPTER 7

The doorbell rang just as Samantha was coming down the stairs. She had indulged in a lazy Saturday morning, as she had been ever since Kathy had moved out. After all, she didn't know how many more opportunities to sleep in she had left.

Her hair was still damp from the shower when she opened the door. Arms raised behind her head in mid-braid when she laid eyes on Dennis.

"Hi," she said, unable to hide her surprise.

"Hi. Listen, do you mind if I come in?"

Before she could even answer, he stepped inside. Noting how brisk it was outside, she was happy enough to close the door.

"I just wanted to apologize for the way I behaved last night." The words in and of themselves seemed sincere, but the way he looked around the house casually as he spoke said otherwise.

Samantha suspected Nancy had something to do with the apology. She finished her braid and quickly tied it off at the end. "Thank you for that. I'll admit, I felt a little attacked about the questions over Christmas."

Dennis murmured an acknowledgment, but studied a painting that hung in the foyer. Something Samantha had recently found in the attic and hung up to try to make the house seem more like hers since Kathy had moved out. She wasn't sure she liked it, though.

"I hope we didn't get off on the wrong foot," Samantha offered. "I would love to be friendly with all of the neighbors. I think it helps everyone if we all just got along."

It was her one and only peace offering. After she and Steven returned home last night, she was about ready to whip up a potion that would *certainly* take care of Dennis. But Steven, as usual, was her voice of reason, suggesting that she play nice with the neighbors' son in the short while he was visiting them. Begrudgingly, she could see his point and agreed to do her part to mend fences.

Because, as everyone knew, nobody makes a great neighbor like a great fence.

"This is a nice house." Dennis moved into the living room and looked around. "All original trim work?"

Samantha followed behind him, noting his snowy boots. "Uh-huh." Using her telepathic abilities, she tried to probe into his mind to read his true intentions, but she hit a wall. It had happened before with strong-willed people. It just meant she needed to keep trying until they let their guard down.

"I can tell," Dennis went on, oblivious to her magic. "And, judging from the funky odor, I'm guessing a lot of the furniture is original too."

Funky odor? Samantha opened her mouth, a snide retort on the tip of her tongue, but she bit it back. "Um, no, actually. The furniture is relatively new. We just appreciate an older style. The smell must be coming from the herbs I had to move inside." She indicated the plants along the windowsills. "I'm always moving them into the sun. It's very important in the winter time."

Dennis followed where she pointed, then looked back at her. "Ah. Right. My parents mentioned that you…grow stuff here."

"I've been trying to, at least." She tried to offer a polite smile, but was sure it probably looked more smug than nice. "After they've reached maturity, I dry the leaves and use them in teas…and stuff." *Potions.*

Her visitor's fingers trailed along the titles on the bookshelf on the wall. "I see your appreciation for old things extends to your literature. These books have been around a while."

"Well, it's an old house," she said. "My family has lived here for a long time. Old things tend to collect here."

He nodded, then glanced through the curtains in the front window. Turning back to Samantha, he pointed across the street. "You know, I didn't mean to come off like a jerk yesterday. I just want to make sure my parents are surrounded by good people."

Samantha's harsh opinion of him softened a little. She could understand that. Protecting the ones you love.

"In my job, I meet a lot of people who look nice on the outside, but are really self-interested back-stabbers."

She raised her eyebrows and did her best to keep her voice even. "Are you suggesting that my family and I are back-stabbers? Because, if you claim that everyone you meet is a back-stabber, then perhaps the problem doesn't lie with everyone else, but with you."

Dennis locked eyes with her and the two exchanged venom wordlessly across the room.

Once again, Samantha tried probing his mind, but her snide comment only strengthened his resolve. Why was he so hard to read? What was he hiding?

"Okay!" Steven's voice carried as he pounded down the squeaky staircase. "What's next on our day of relaxation? Because I have a few idea—oh, sorry. Didn't realize we had company. Dennis! Hi!" He stepped into the living room and offered his hand for their guest to shake.

Dennis held his stare with Samantha for a moment longer. Finally, he turned to Steven and offered a tight smile. "Steven."

Slowly, Samantha's husband lowered his hand, recognizing that this was not a friendly encounter.

"Did you, uh—" Steven looked to Samantha in an effort to read the room, but even he couldn't decipher what she was thinking. "—did you want to stay for lunch or something? It's a little early to eat, but if you're hungry..."

"No, that's okay," Dennis said. "I should get back to my parents. I'll see you around." Without a look in Samantha's direction, he turned to the door and let himself out.

When they were alone, Steven asked, "What was that about?"

"I'm not sure, exactly," she admitted. "All I know is that there's something about him that I really don't like."

CHAPTER 8

- MAY 1988 -
- ANNAPOLIS, MD -

Dennis and Maggie stumbled onto the sailboat docked at the marina. They had barely taken their hands off each other since they had left the bar. There was so much to celebrate—Dennis graduating from the Naval Academy; Maggie getting her first job. Despite the fact that the two had just met only a few hours ago, there was no denying their desire to celebrate with each other—or the passion between them.

"You sure your old man doesn't mind?" Dennis asked when they fumbled into the small cabin belowdeck. There was a small lounge with a kitchenette tucked into one corner. Through one door led to a closet, another to a small bathroom, and the third led to the small sleeping area. Dennis had his eyes on that.

"No," Maggie murmured between kisses. She fumbled with

the buttons on her blouse. "He's out of town. Gone for the weekend." She pulled her shirt off and then started for his.

"No brothers or anyone who're going to throw me overboard in the buff?"

She pulled away, her chest heaving with each breath she took. "Look. You seem nervous. Are you sure you want to do this?"

Dennis took one look at her and nodded. "Oh yeah. I'm sure."

"Then what's the deal?"

He shrugged.

"Is it that bullshit the guys in the bar were talking about? The shipwrecks in the yard?"

"That wasn't bullshit. That was on the news."

The talk of the town was that a lot of local sailors had been having freak shipwrecks before they even left the boatyard. Brand new vessels suddenly taking on water, or other sinking just as they pulled into port after traveling up the coast. And that wasn't to mention the non-existent fishing stock that seemed to disappear overnight.

Dennis didn't have his own boat and he only fished once in a while, but even he had to admit that the changes were unsettling. *Something* was going on and it didn't look good.

She shot him a look. "They said it was pirates. In Annapolis."

"Well, okay, maybe not *pirates*, but..." He ended his

argument up with a shrug.

"So why don't you do us both a favor and go up to make sure the coast is clear." She nodded to the small bathroom. "I'm going to freshen up. Make yourself at home." Maggie gave him a smirk as she disappeared into the small room.

When she was gone, Dennis walked up the few steps and stuck his head out just above deck. Beneath the lights of the marina, he couldn't see anyone. And all he could hear were the sound of the water lapping up between the boat and dock, rocking the boat slightly.

Satisfied that they were alone, he returned to the cabin and pulled off his shirt the rest of the way. He kicked off his boots and set them off to the side.

The cabin was beautiful. Dennis wondered if Maggie's father had both it new or restored it to its original beauty—not that he wanted to think of her father much tonight.

He stepped into the small bedroom and took in the size of the bed. It was a double, which was small for everyday standards, but would do just fine for the type of night Dennis and Maggie had in mind.

One of the storage drawers beneath the bed sat askew in its tray. Dennis knelt down and tried to pull it out, but it was jammed. He gave it some extra force and finally pulled it out. Before he had a chance to set the drawer back on its tray, something caught his eye.

It was tucked—hidden—in the spot directly underneath the

drawer. If the drawer had been working properly, he never would've even known it was there. It was a small, tattered leather-bound notebook.

Dennis reached for it and opened it. Each page had handwritten notes front and back. Some of the handwriting in the beginning of the book were faded or written in such curly script that he couldn't make out what it said. But as he flipped through the pages, they became clearer—and Dennis became more worried.

"How to draw up a storm," read one. "How to drown someone without water," read another. A third one really scared him, as he remembered the elaborate claims his fellow sailors had made: "How to sing a siren's song."

Below each entry was a list of ingredients—herbs, mostly, but also some everyday items, as well as some he had never heard of. Some entries contained short poems beneath. Dennis began to read one, when he heard something behind him.

"What are you doing?" Maggie asked. She wore a loose-fitting robe that she clutched tighter around herself.

Dennis rose to his feet and held up the notebook. "What is this?" He approached her slowly, trying to close the distance between them without her realizing.

"I asked you first."

"Is this your father's?" He indicated her robe. "Or yours?"

She looked down at what she was wearing and crossed her arms over herself. She took a step backward, but refused to look

Dennis in the eyes.

"Seems I'm not the first one you've had here." He tossed the notebook on the small dining table as he passed.

Maggie flung an arm toward the staircase leading above. "I want you to leave."

Dennis snatched her arm and pulled her close. She let out a yelp, but gritted her teeth when they were face-to-face.

"What have you been doing here with that book of—" He stopped as something else caught his eye.

Maggie's robe had slipped down off her shoulder when he grabbed her, revealing a tattoo of an upside down triangle with a line beneath it. He had seen the same mark on several of the pages in the notebook.

"What is that?"

She glared down at her shoulder. "It's a tattoo. Thought you and your boys would've known all about that, since it seems you like to talk."

He gripped her wrist tighter and slapped her with the back of his free hand. "Don't treat me like I'm stupid!"

"Ow!" she shouted. "You're hurting me! Let me go! Help! Somebody help me! I'm in Mitch Forester's—"

Her cries for help were silenced as Dennis tackled her to the ground, a hand over her mouth.

Crawling on top of her, he pinned her arms down with his legs and put the hand that wasn't covering her mouth on her shoulder to cover the tattoo.

"Are you the one who has been causing shipwrecks in the harbor?" Slowly, he pulled his hand away from her mouth to allow her to answer.

"Go to hell," she sneered.

The next thing Dennis knew, he was sailing up in the air, hitting the low ceiling in the cabin.

When he crashed back down on the floor, he scurried to his feet and looked at her with wide eyes. "What the hell was that?" He noticed that he was now blocking the exit. This woman—this *freak*—wasn't going to get away from him.

They both stood, sizing each other up in the small cabin. Both of their chests were heaving now, but for different reasons than they were only minutes ago.

Finally, Dennis broke the silence. "Are you…some kind…" He shrugged. "I don't know, *witch*?"

She held out her hands to ward him off. "I can explain."

Dennis didn't offer her a chance to explain. He had seen enough. With one quick motion, he grabbed her wrist and dropped her to the floor. Within another second, he was on top of her, his hands pressed to her throat. If she couldn't talk, she couldn't cast any spells on him. And if she couldn't breathe, she couldn't use her powers on him.

At least, he hoped.

Maggie fought to free his grip from her neck. Her eyes were wide with terror. Her painted nails dug into his flesh, drawing blood.

He loosened one hand to readjust, but it was enough for her to use her power on him again. It didn't have the same effect as before. This time, only his hand flailed up in the air above him, but he kept his hold on her.

Quickly recovering, he brought his hands together around her throat and felt his aggression take over. It was like he was a different person when he got like this. He wasn't himself. He wasn't thinking clearly. All he wanted to do was hurt someone.

As Maggie continued to struggle against his grip and Dennis's own anger intensified, he lifted her off the floor, only to slam her back down. Her head hit the hardwood with a solid thud that made her eyes bulge out. He did it again. And again. Over and over until her grip on his hands went slack and her eyes rolled back.

Only then did he realize what he had just done.

He released her and scrambled to his feet. Maggie didn't move. She lay there, crumpled on the floor in what had once been a seductive gown. Now it lay limply on her broken body.

Dennis felt bile rise to his throat, but he swallowed it down. Now was not the time to get sick. He needed to act.

First, he needed to get rid of the body, then he needed to clean up the scene, and finally, he needed to get the hell out of dodge and hope that nobody saw him enter the boat with her.

For a moment, Dennis couldn't pry his eyes off of Maggie's body. But the thought of what could happen to him if anyone found out what he'd done—despite what he had known about her and what she could do—pushed him into motion.

Maggie was a witch and she deserved to die. And now he needed to pick up the pieces that she had left.

CHAPTER 9

We need to talk," Kathy announced as she walked right through the front door of Samantha's house. That thought was something she was still adjusting to. The fact that this house was now only Samantha's. Sure, Kathy would always have a sense of ownership over it, but eventually she'd have to get in the habit of at least notifying her sister that she was coming over before she did.

Today was not one of those days, though.

Kathy stopped short in the foyer when she didn't see anyone around. "Hello? Sam? Steven?"

"Hmm?" Samantha murmured from the living room.

She followed the sound of her sister's voice.

Samantha held a mug of steaming tea between her hands.

She stood at the window, watching the house across the street through the sheer curtains.

"What are you doing?" Kathy asked. "Spying on the neighbors?"

"Actually, yeah," the older sister responded without taking her eyes off of her target. "I'm watching the Kors' house."

"That old couple?" Kathy came up beside Samantha and took a look for herself. There wasn't much to see. The street had been tinted white with the liberal use of salt since the snow had begun to fall. And to think that it wasn't technically even winter yet. Through the blanket of snow, every house had cleared paths for driveways, doorways, and sidewalks, leaving mounds alongside each clearing.

Other than that, the street was quiet. The temperature was too cold to enjoy being out in and the snow prevented any minor work to be done outside. And even with the overcast day, there was no need for anyone to have their lights on. The Kors house, among all the others on the street, sat silently, withholding all of its secrets to the world.

"Gerald and Nancy," Samantha told her. "Their son Dennis came home to visit. He's in the Navy."

"I didn't realize they had a son."

"They have two, apparently. Maybe more."

"Hmm," Kathy said, uninterested. "The things you don't know about your neighbors." Having grown bored of watching the street, Kathy turned to her sister. "Anyway, I need to tell you something big."

Samantha finally glanced over at her. "Did something happen?"

"Sort of," Kathy started, then quickly added, "Nothing bad. Not witchy-bad, at least. Do you remember Michael?"

"Jeremy's roommate?" Samantha took a sip of her tea. She made a face and then took a step toward the end table near the couch to set it down.

"Yep. They're friends—or they were. I guess Michael said even he's had enough of Jeremy lately. I guess he's gone off on the deep end or something, I don't know. It's actually really sad and—"

"Kathy, you were getting to the point in here somewhere?"

"Oh, right. I ran into Michael last night and we got talking. We went up to my apartment and—are you okay?"

Samantha leaned against the wall, her brow furrowed, and rubbed her belly. "Yeah, I'm fine. My stomach is just kind of turning. Nancy's lasagna from last night hasn't been sitting well with me all morning. Apparently the baby doesn't like it." She waved Kathy on. "I'm fine. I'm listening."

"Anyway, when we were up at my apartment, I started feeling—I don't know—attracted to Michael, almost. I can't really tell if it was just nostalgia or what, but there was definitely something there. Or I guess it could've been the booze." She expected a reaction from Samantha about the alcohol, but her sister was still rubbing her belly. "Are you sure you're okay?"

Samantha shook her head slightly and stepped to the couch to lean on. She started taking deeper breaths.

"Sam, you're kind of scaring me. Is it the baby?"

Another moment passed before Samantha stood up again, the pain on her face having faded. "It's gone."

"What's gone? What's going on?"

"Just discomfort or something." Samantha motioned downward.

"Like you need to go to the bathroom?"

Samantha shot her a look. "No, Kathy. I know what that feels like. Just go on. You were getting drunk with Michael?"

"Not intentionally," Kathy clarified. "It just kind of happened. Especially because I had already had a couple drinks down at the bar before we went upstairs. Anyway, my memory is kind of sketchy after that."

Samantha rolled her eyes. She always hated Kathy's more carefree lifestyle and her blasé attitude to drinking and dating.

"All I know is that this morning I woke up and Michael was in bed with me," Kathy finished.

"You slept with him?"

"I don't *think* so..."

Exhaling loudly, Samantha conveyed her displeasure without a single word.

"Even if I did, it's *Michael*. It's not like it was some stranger from the bar. I mean, I've known this guy for as long as I've known Jeremy!"

"Fair enough, but still."

"I know."

Samantha released another deep breath, whether it was from Kathy's story or her own discomfort was uncertain. "So do you like Michael like that?"

Kathy shrugged. "I don't *not* like him. Before last night, though, I never really thought about him in that way."

"Well, how did you feel when you woke up next to him this morning? Happy? Embarrassed? Shameful?"

"I don't know. I was freaked out, but I think that was more because I didn't remember what had happened. After we had put our clothes on—"

Samantha dropped her arms and shifted her steps. "You were *naked*?"

"I wasn't! He was just in his underwear."

"Oh, because *that* makes it better!"

"Again, even if we *did* sleep together, he's not a stranger."

Another sigh from Samantha. "You're right. Sorry. What did he say when he left?"

"That's the thing. He stayed and I made breakfast."

"And that was okay?" Samantha glanced out the window, but when nothing interesting caught her eye, she turned back to her sister.

"Yeah. It was like he had stopped over to chat. It was actually pretty relaxed, considering how the morning started. I do remember that he kissed me last night, which he blames on the booze, but I have my doubts."

"Well, it sounds like you two like each other. So what's the problem?"

Kathy groaned and flopped back on the couch. "The problem is that I feel like the biggest cliché for sleeping with my ex's best friend! I mean, what is Jeremy going to think? Not that I *care* what he thinks, but I don't want to hurt him either. What do you think?" She waited for Samantha to respond. When she didn't, Kathy sat up and saw that her sister was hunched over again. "Sam, please take a seat. You're scaring me."

Samantha's face was contorted in pain as she bent over. She leaned one hand on the couch and the other hand on her belly.

Kathy got to her feet and came to her sister's side. "What can I do? What's going on?"

"Steven!" Samantha shouted. "Steven, get in here!"

Her husband came rushing in from the kitchen. His eyes were wide with worry. "What is it? What's going on?"

"Call the doctor," Samantha said. "I think I'm going into labor."

CHAPTER 10

The constant smile on Nancy Kors' face as she played her next turn of rummy was enough for Dennis to rest assured in his decision to come home before Christmas. He would miss the holiday, but at least he would be able to see his parents close enough to Christmas. That was going to have to be enough.

"I went over to apologize to Samantha this morning." Dennis picked up a card at his next turn and studied it.

"That was nice. She really is a nice woman—all of them are. Steven and Kathy too."

"So you've spent a lot of time with them?" Dennis laid out his piles and then discarded.

"Not much, actually. They're so busy and we're just an old

couple, but they always wave and say hello with a smile. Kathy brought over a package last summer when it was accidentally delivered to their house."

"That was nice."

"I thought so too." She studied her cards. "Hmm…I'm running out of options here."

"Perhaps you should just forfeit," Dennis said with a smirk.

"I didn't raise any quitters because I'm not a quitter," she said with a wink before placing her discard down. "I hope after your visit to Samantha that you saw for yourself that there's nothing to worry about with them."

"I know. I was just taken by surprise by everything I heard about them. Bad first impression, I guess."

Nancy nodded. "Yes, it was. Like I said, they're all very nice."

"And all of those other…*oddities*, as Dad put it, they don't bother you?"

She sighed heavily. "They can be a bit strange in some of their habits, yes. But who doesn't have their own quirks?"

"Strange in what way?"

"Would you stop, Dennis? My neighbors are perfectly fine."

He shrugged and played his next turn. "Just curious, that's all."

His mother studied him a minute before saying, "They purchase some interesting things."

"Interesting in what way?"

"Well, I remember when your father and I first moved to the

street, I brought over a plate of cookies to introduce ourselves. Samantha was bringing in the groceries. I offered to help and caught a peek inside one of the paper bags—oh, the stench from that thing!"

"She told me she likes to grow her own herbs."

"So this must've been before she started growing her own, then. I asked her what it was for and she told me she liked to dabble in the kitchen."

Dennis nodded, even though he wasn't buying the excuse Samantha had given his mother. There was more to that house. Something they were hiding. Something big, and possibly dangerous.

"Nothing else?"

"Sweetie, you know I don't like to gossip."

"Is it gossip if it dies with me?" he asked. "Seriously, Mom, who am I going to tell? It's not like *I* live in the neighborhood."

"That is true." She sighed again. "Well, all right. On a different occasion, I waved to Kathy as I was getting our paper from the end of the driveway—this must've been the summer time. Kathy was just coming home—she doesn't have a car of her own, see. So she takes the bus. The bus stop is just down the street on Cherry. Anyway, she was carrying this thing that was wrapped in paper."

"What thing?"

"I'm not sure. It was large. Heavy. Almost looked like a bowl, perhaps. She claimed it was an antique she had restored, but I had never seen anything like it. Anyway, there were other things with her as well. Trinkets and jewelry and such. But it all seemed so gaudy and I've never seen either of the girls wearing any of it."

"Interesting."

"I'm sure it was nothing," she insisted. "Probably just garage sale finds that ended up in the trash after a second thought."

"Probably," Dennis offered. He still wasn't convinced that everything was so innocent across the street, but he didn't want to upset his mother. Instead, he changed the subject to something else that bothered him. "So do you like living here?"

"We do." With several sets, she laid down the remaining cards in her hand and then raised her fists up. "I win!"

"Surprise, surprise," Gerald said as he came in from the living room. The TV still blared from the doorway with commercials advertising other old movies to watch. "You better back out now, son, or you'll be locked into another card game before you know it."

"I only do that with you because you care more about that TV than you do me!" she said with a laugh.

"That's because the TV doesn't give me attitude or spend my money!"

"That TV doesn't make you dinner or do your laundry, either."

Gerald grumbled and escaped into the kitchen for a drink. As he passed back through the living room, Dennis said, "Dad, what is your favorite and least favorite thing about this house?"

"What the hell kind of question is that?" he asked.

"Just answer it!" Nancy snapped. "I'm curious to know too."

"My least favorite is the size of the damn place. Too big for the two of us, if you ask me, but your mother loves the old charm and I like the quiet neighborhood."

"And your favorite?"

Gerald smiled. "Hands-down, how cheap this place was."

"And that's because of the murders, right?"

Nancy scoffed and rose to her feet. "I don't want to talk about this. I try not to think about those poor people in the basement. Gives me the creeps whenever I'm down there doing the laundry."

"I put extra lights down there."

"Lights can only do so much, Gerald. I'm going to fix something for lunch." She disappeared into the kitchen.

"Do you know who it was who was murdered here?" Dennis asked his father quietly after Nancy was gone.

Gerald sighed and took a seat at the end of the table. "No, I don't. But you could probably ask the girls across the street. There's a good chance they knew the previous owners."

"Were they friends?"

"I don't know. As far as I know, the sisters have lived there forever."

"Do you think they were here the night of the murders?"

Gerald rubbed his stubbly chin. "Again, it's possible. The

previous owners were throwing a Halloween party here when it happened—or rather, when the captives were found in the basement."

"Since they're into such weird things, I would think Halloween would be right up their alley."

"I'm not really sure about that one, son."

Dennis motioned through the front window across the street. "Well, they obviously don't decorate for Christmas because they don't celebrate it, so do they decorate for Halloween? That would say whether they liked the holiday—if you can call Halloween a holiday."

"They did have some decorations up," Gerald said. "But that doesn't mean they were here at the party last year."

Nancy emerged from the kitchen with a tray stocked with food and dishes. "Lunch is served!"

Gerald nudged his son. "She's only doing this because you're here."

"And you better soak it all up," she told her husband. "You can make your own lunch, you know."

Dennis smiled when she set the tray in the middle of the table. There was luncheon meat, bread, condiments, and a bag of chips all spread out. "This looks great, Mom. Thank you."

"Of course, dear. I wasn't sure what kind of sandwich you wanted, so I brought everything we have."

"This is perfect. Thanks."

Gerald dug in and started spreading mayonnaise on his

sandwich. He looked up and pointed with the knife across the street. "Speak of the devil, where do you think they're going?"

Dennis looked and saw Samantha, Kathy, and Steven all rushing down the front steps to the car. Samantha walked considerably slower, clutching her belly with one hand and her husband's arm with the other as she made her way down the steps.

"Oh!" Nancy cheered. "I wonder if she's going to have the baby!"

CHAPTER 11

Do you need more water?" Steven asked his wife.

"I can get it." Kathy took the pink pitcher from him. "Cover her feet. They're sticking out."

"Got it." He moved around to the end of the bed and tucked the blankets under his wife's feet. "Anything else you need, honey?"

"I need you two to relax," Samantha said. She was perched in the bed in her room at the hospital. The nurses had set her up nicely, explaining that the doctor would be in periodically to check on her and discuss with her the options available. They had already had a lot of the important conversations about the birth back at his office a few weeks ago, but the nurse explained that he liked to double check in case women changed their minds when arrival day came.

Kathy returned with the pitcher full of water, as well as a bucket full of ice chips. "I thought you might want to snack on these." She set the two containers on the little overhang table by the bed, then reached behind Samantha to fluff the pillows.

Samantha sat up and swatted her sister away. "Knock it off! I'm fine."

"I just want to make sure you're comfortable," Kathy said.

With a sigh, Samantha said, "I know. And I appreciate it. I do. But you're driving me nuts! I'm having a baby, I'm not an invalid."

"Sorry," Steven said. "But if you need anything—"

"What I need is a little bit of space and for you two to act a little more casual," she said. "All of this hovering you're doing is just making me stressed out and uncomfortable."

"Sorry," Kathy echoed.

Steven slumped into a chair beside Kathy. "I just feel so helpless."

"If you want to help, you can go find my doctor so he can tell me how soon I can get the drugs pumped into my body," Samantha said. "With the way these contractions have been, I sure don't want to feel the actual birth."

He shot to his feet. "I'm on it."

When he was gone, Samantha rolled her eyes with a grin. "I love him."

"Even though he's driving you crazy?" Kathy asked.

"It's only because he cares."

"Just make sure you remind him that you love him. He just wants to feel included."

"I know. And I will." Samantha smirked. "It'll be better when I'm numb."

"Do you really want to be drugged up for your first baby?" Kathy asked.

"If I'm not, then this will be my *only* baby." She smiled at her joke, but when her sister didn't, she added, "What's up?"

Kathy faked a smile. "Nothing."

"Come on, Kathy. You can't fool me. I know something is on your mind."

"Well, yeah, but the baby is much more pressing than anything I've got going on."

"The baby is taking his or her sweet old time," Samantha said. "Besides, I could use a distraction from all this fuss over me."

Kathy continued to sit and play with her cuticles.

"Is it about Michael?"

She shrugged. "I'm just worried that I screwed things up with a good friend. I mean, even if nothing *technically* happened between us last night, a line was crossed that we can't go back from."

"You're still not sure if you slept with him?"

"I'm pretty sure we didn't. But I do know we kissed. And I know you may be shocked to hear this, but I don't just go around kissing anyone. At least, not often."

Samantha smiled. Even though she and her sister were very different, she admired Kathy's freer nature. Samantha sometimes envied that, thinking of herself as too stuffy and boring a lot of times. More often than she ever admitted, she tried to view things through Kathy's perspective.

"You should just talk to Michael," Samantha said. "Just get it out in the open and have that uncomfortable conversation so you both know where you stand."

Kathy made a face. "Easier said than done."

"True. But think about it this way: if Michael's really as good of a friend as you say he is, then he's probably worrying about the same thing too. And he's going to agree that you two *do* need to talk about what happened—or didn't happen. He'll understand."

All Kathy could do was nod.

Before the conversation could go on any further, Steven walked into the room with Samantha's doctor. He wore a white lab coat, adorned with his name tag clipped to the same pocket that held a number of pens in it. Around his neck was a stethoscope. He pulled Samantha's chart from the end of her bed and looked it over.

"Good afternoon, Mrs. Harper," he said as he read over the clipboard. "How are you feeling?"

"Not bad, considering." Samantha smiled at her husband, silently thanking him for delivering on his promise. "The contractions are killer, though."

Dr. Mendon looked up and nodded. "Unfortunately, the contractions are only going to get worse. Your husband said you were asking about the anesthesia we had talked about?"

"Yes! How soon can I get some?" she asked. "The last contraction was brutal."

"Let's take a look." He looked to Kathy. "Would you mind stepping out?"

"She can stay," Samantha said. "She's my sister."

Dr. Mendon smiled at her and offered his hand. "Nice to meet you."

She shook it. "Likewise. I'm Kathy, Samantha's younger sister."

He stepped over to the sink to wash his hands. "You must be very excited about becoming an aunt."

"Very," she said. "Can't wait to meet my little niece or nephew."

Dr. Mendon dried his hands and then pulled on some rubber gloves. He adjusted the stirrups for Samantha. "Let's see how long we have to wait to meet the little guy or girl." He lifted the sheet at the end of Samantha's bed.

Samantha stared at the ceiling, feeling completely exposed. She knew it was only going to get worse, but she was also glad that she had Steven and Kathy by her side.

"Hmm," Dr. Mendon said when he pulled away.

Samantha readjusted on the bed, setting her legs back down

on the mattress. "What is it?"

"It looks like you're only two centimeters dilated."

"And how much does she need to be to deliver?" Steven asked.

"Ten," Dr. Mendon told him. He looked back at Samantha. "I'm afraid you still have a long way to go."

CHAPTER 12

The lock on the back door of the Harper house was easy to pick. Dennis had learned how to do it from a friend back at the base. Part of the "unofficial" training he went through in the Navy.

With the door opened, he crept inside the dark house. Lucky for him, it was now getting dark as early as four o'clock, which meant he used the early dusk to his advantage.

Stepping into the kitchen, he tried to spot anything out of the ordinary. Dennis had a curiosity about Samantha, Kathy, and, by extension, Steven. Based on everything his parents had told him about them, there was something that didn't sit right with him. He didn't want to go so far as to say he was *worried,* but he did want to make sure that his parents weren't living next to dangerous people.

Whatever had happened over a year ago in his parents' basement prior to them buying the house made him wonder if the sisters had anything to do with it.

It was a stretch, he understood that much, but what he knew about what the sisters didn't sit right with him. The avoidance of the subject at dinner, the peculiarities about the two women, and the fact that there was a chance that they had been at that party that night. Dennis had a gut feeling that they were bad news. Maybe they even had something to do with the actual murders and kidnapping.

The only way he was going to clear his mind was to scope out their house. It wasn't like he was going to break anything. He wanted to leave no trace that he was there at all. But he had to learn more about them.

Dennis first went to the kitchen cabinets. He found dishes, pots, pans, skillets, and food. Just like every other house in America. The drawers revealed nothing, either. Silverware, measuring spoons, potato masher, mixing beaters, junk drawer, stacks of how-to manuals from various appliances. All of it was so…*ordinary*.

He crossed the kitchen and checked another row of cabinets and stumbled on something that definitely *wasn't* in every other house. Tucked up in a high cabinet was a plastic tote filled with baggies of some kind of dried leaves.

Dennis's first thought was pot, based on what his own

experience in college had been. But then he remembered what Samantha had told him about growing her own herbs and figured that that was probably what he was looking at.

The whole cabinet reeked of the stuff, though.

He put it back and opened the other door to the same cabinet, which revealed an even stranger find. Little vials of liquid sat in a row, filling almost the entire left side of the cabinet. Each of the tiny glass bottles had a piece of tape with something written on them in marker, like his mother did with leftovers in the freezer.

Dennis picked several of them up and read each of the tags out loud to himself.

"To protect. To heal. To erase memories."

What the heck were these things?

Unscrewing the cap of one, he took a quick sniff and immediately pulled it away. Whatever was inside smelled foul. He recapped it and placed the vials back in the cabinet.

Okay, he thought to himself. *Weird things in the cabinet doesn't make them murderers. Just makes them very strange.*

Unsatisfied with his finds in the kitchen, Dennis moved on to the rest of the house. Through the doorway brought him to the dining room, which had a door to the sunroom and a large cased opening to the foyer, off of which sat the living room. He had only taken a brief glance at everything in the living room earlier when he came to apologize to Samantha, but from what he'd seen he hadn't noticed anything out of the ordinary.

Besides, if they were hiding something, they wouldn't be hiding it out in the common areas downstairs.

Off of the foyer was the staircase with a intricate wooden banister. He glanced up it, considering if *he* was the weird one. He was trespassing in their house when he knew they were out. It was illegal and if his supervisors found out…

Dennis shook his head. He loved his job, but he'd risk it if it meant protecting his family. He wasn't about to go back to work and leave his parents vulnerable to potentially dangerous people living right across the street. Not after he himself had been asking Samantha personal questions that could come back to bite his parents in the ass.

The steps were creaky, which was predictable for such an old house—his parents' house across the street was creaky too—but in the dark silence, each squeak of the floorboards felt like an alarm going off, notifying everyone that he was somewhere he shouldn't.

At the top of the stairs, he noted the small landing with several rooms off of it. The first door on the left was the bathroom. At the end of the hall, Dennis was momentarily surprised to find a nursery. The idea of a baby was such a basic human, nurturing thing that didn't quite fit in line with the narrative he was building against the sisters that said they were murderers.

But, of course, they had discussed the baby at dinner last night. Not to mention, the whole reason Dennis was alone in their house was because they were off *having* the baby.

His stomach turned as he thought about a baby joining this family of weirdos. Certainly it would be much better suited in a more normal family. If the baby grew up with Samantha, then she would bend him or her to her own influence.

Perhaps Steven, who seemed more like a reluctant accomplice, could offset Samantha's pull. But no matter how strong of an influence Steven was to the child, Samantha's pull would be stronger as the mother.

The room next to the nursery was empty. Again, this surprised Dennis at first until he remembered the comment about Kathy having just recently moved out.

Dennis moved on to the last room upstairs, which was Samantha and Steven's room. It was fully furnished, with a queen-sized bed in the center, flanked by two oak nightstands and dressers on opposite sides of the room. To the left were a set of closets taking up the whole wall.

He went to work, checking the closets, dressers, nightstands, under the mattress, under the bed. Everywhere.

Nothing.

Grumbling to himself, he stepped back into the hall.

Should I go back and try not to think about these people living across the street from Mom and Dad? he wondered to himself. *Or keep digging while I'm here until I find something?*

The urge to keep digging was greater. In fact, he decided, he would search the attic and the basement if he had to. All of the hiding places in this old house.

Returning to the empty bedroom, he scoped out the floor for any loose boards that might be disguising a hidden compartment.

Nothing. Every single board was securely fastened.

He tried tugging at the intricate heating vent, but it was screwed in tight.

When he was about to give up and move on, he realized he had missed the obvious. The closet door sat closed, containing another hiding space. Maybe multiple hiding spaces.

"Jackpot!" he cheered when he opened the door. Sitting on the shelf in the closet sat a large, leather-bound book.

It was different than the tomes stored on the bookshelves in the living room. This one was heartier, although more worn than the others. What caught Dennis's eye, though, was the title: *The Art of Magic*.

Flipping through the pages revealed spells, incantations, and potion recipes calling for the herbs he found in the kitchen. But there was more: entries on witches, wizards, demons, sorcerers, all kinds of mythical creatures and beings.

Finally, he stopped on a page that revealed exactly what he had been looking for. A large ornate diagram listed the births, deaths, and relationships between several "witches," as the book called them. Sitting at the bottom of the family tree were the names "Samantha" and "Kathy."

Dennis leaned against the wall for support as the realization struck him. His parents weren't just living across the street from murderers. These women were witches. And they were about to bring another one into the world.

CHAPTER 13

It won't be that bad," Steven said to his wife after the doctor left. "I'm sure things will move quicker the closer you get."

"Says the man who is not about to push a *person* out of them," Samantha snapped. She sat with her arms crossed, annoyed at the news that the doctor had delivered.

"I'm just trying to look on the bright side," he said.

"The bright side? The longer I sit here, the longer I have to endure the pain of childbirth."

"But one day of pain for a lifetime with our child?" he offered.

"One day? *One day?* Do you know what they're about to do to me when this baby comes? Trust me, this is *not* going to be a *one day* thing." She rolled her eyes.

Kathy let out a sigh. She had been quiet up until this point, leaving Steven room to comfort his wife. But as the exchange went on, and he only made things worse, she knew she had to say something.

"Sam, I know you're frustrated. I would be too. But there's nothing that can be done about it. That's just something you're going to have to get over—and quick. There's no sense stewing about it and causing all kinds of stress on your body. That's only going to make the pain worse and it'll ruin the moment of meeting your baby too. Besides, all those stress hormones are going right to the baby right now. Do you really want him or her to be feeling that?"

"So I'm just supposed to turn off this stress like a switch?" Samantha asked. "I'll remember that advice when it's *you* sitting in this bed and not me."

That didn't quite go as Kathy had planned. "Just try to focus on the joy of meeting your baby."

"The way I see it, there's nothing enjoyable about this."

Kathy and Steven exchanged glances. Samantha's mood swings had been getting worse over the last few weeks of her pregnancy. They knew it was hormones, but it was still annoying to deal with. If anything, Samantha's attitude had brought Kathy and Steven closer together as they leaned on each other to complain about her. Common enemy and everything. The last month or so had actually been easier on Kathy since she had moved out.

"Honey, why don't you try to get some sleep while you can?" Steven suggested. "If it's going to be a while still, you're probably going to be up all night. You're going to need your strength when the time comes."

"That's a good idea," Kathy added.

"Oh, sure. So not only am I supposed to think about a tiny human ripping me to shreds on its entry into the world, I'm also supposed to enjoy a nice relaxing sleep as this child claws its way out of me? Hey, no problem!"

"Then sit there and stew," Steven snapped back. "At least we're suggesting ideas. You're just bitching and making it worse for yourself and for everyone who has to deal with you."

Kathy bit back her lip. That certainly wasn't the best thing to say to a woman in labor, but surprisingly, Samantha didn't offer a retort. Maybe she had realized that there was truth behind Steven's words.

The room was tense until a nurse knocked on the door before stepping in. She was young, blonde, and probably still within her first year of nursing judging by the pep in her step. A lot of the other nurses faked it—and faked it well. Their enthusiasm had been beaten out of them long ago by long shifts, brutal patients, and strange policies from administration.

"Hello there!" she beamed with a smile. "Just wanted to check on your vitals and see how you're doing." She stepped to one of the machines beside Samantha's bed and made notations on her chart.

"I'm okay," Samantha said.

"She's frustrated," Kathy added. "About how long it's going to take."

The nurse nodded. From the ID badge hanging around her neck, Kathy saw her name was Debbie. "Yeah, I know it can be hard."

"Is there anything that can help speed up the process?" Steven asked. "She's in a lot of discomfort."

Debbie scrunched her face. "Not really. The baby is going to come when its ready."

"So there's nothing I can do?" Samantha's shoulders slumped.

"Well, sometimes moving around can help, but—"

Samantha pulled back the sheet and began lowering her feet to the floor before Debbie could finish.

Kathy and Steven jumped up, although Debbie was right by Samantha's side. The nurse clutched Samantha's wrist to steady her, then rolled her IV drip closer.

"*But,*" Debbie continued, "I would be careful how much moving you're doing and what kind. Not splits or jumps or anything crazy like that."

"Walking is okay, though?" Samantha asked.

With a smile, Debbie nodded. "Yes. Walking is perfectly fine. Just…bring Dad along with you, just in case."

Samantha wheeled her IV bag alongside her and headed for the door. Steven raced after her.

When they were gone, Kathy turned to Debbie and asked, "So there's nothing medically that can be done?"

"The doctor *could* induce labor, but from what I'm seeing on her chart I don't think that's likely," Debbie said. "Your sister is progressing just fine. The baby is simply taking its time."

CHAPTER 14

Jeopardy! played on the TV in the Kors' living room. Gerald watched with interest while Nancy only casually played attention. She had pulled out her knitting, which was stored in a wicker basket beside the couch.

"I wish I knew whether Samantha was having a boy or a girl," she murmured. "Green just doesn't have the same effect as a blue or pink blanket."

"I'm sure they'll appreciate it regardless of the color," Gerald told her, just before turning up the sound on the TV.

"Who was Thomas Jefferson?" one of the contestants answered.

Dennis sat on the opposite side of the room in a lounge chair, not paying any attention to the game show. *The Art of*

WITCH HUNTER

Magic lay in his lap and he read each page carefully. The further he got into the book, though, the more it scared him.

The incantations included anything from changing your appearance to manipulating another person. The potion recipes called for herbs and spices, some of them even poisonous. Other rituals required blood to spill—was that what the sisters were doing in this very house at that Halloween party? Is that why those people were murdered, and other people taken hostage? What kind of ritual were they doing?

The profiles on demons, witches, and other creatures seemed like complete fiction. Although many of the more demonic ones had spells written below the profile that usually started with "to kill." Were these women—these *witches*—really capable of killing another living thing? What stopped them from killing anyone who pissed them off?

"So…your neighbors," Dennis started.

"What is the ozone layer?" one of the contestants on the TV asked.

"Huh?" Gerald glanced over at his son before returning to the TV. "Did you say something?"

"Samantha and…Kathy, is it?"

Nancy nodded, her eyes still on her knitting. "Yes, dear, what about them?"

"If they're sisters, what happened to their parents?"

"Oh, I'm not sure," his mother replied. "As far as I know, it's just the two of them. They haven't spoken about their parents much. I have a feeling that they're both dead since the house is in the girls' names."

"And they have no other family around?"

"I'm not really sure." Nancy finally set her knitting in her lap and looked across the room. "Why the sudden interest in those two?"

"Do you have a crush?" Gerald teased.

"I think Kathy may be single," Nancy added.

Dennis decided to play it off as a crush. That was the only way that would make sense as to why he was asking so many questions about them. "Well, you know how it is. I spend most of my time with the guys back at base. When I see a pretty girl, it piques my interest."

Nancy smiled. "Well then, in that case, I know they work. Samantha, of course, is an accountant, as she mentioned yesterday at dinner. I'm not sure where Kathy works. I do know that she doesn't live there anymore, but she still seems to be over there an awful lot."

"And they like to party?"

"How are we supposed to know that?" Gerald asked. "It's not like they're inviting these old geezers out to the bars with them."

Nancy swatted at her husband. "The lights in the house are usually on Friday and Saturday nights, so I would say they're not ones for too many late-night outings. Are you interested in asking Kathy out sometime?"

"Maybe. I was just thinking, you said Samantha and Kathy were here? That night of the Halloween party last year?"

Both Gerald and Nancy's faces dropped.

"Oh," she said. "I—I think so. That's what I've gathered. I don't know many details."

"What *do* you know?"

"Well, like I told you earlier, there were a couple people held hostage—"

Gerald used the arm of the couch to haul himself to his feet. "I don't want to hear this! It's Christmas! Let's not wallow in the bad memories." He stalked off into the kitchen.

When he was gone, Dennis turned to his mother. "Sorry. I'm just curious. It's kind of a weird situation."

"I know, dear, but it's not something we like to think about a lot. Your father makes jokes, but it does get to him. I know it weighs on my mind."

"Just one more question, and then I'll drop it forever. Do you know who the responding officer was that night?"

CHAPTER 15

Out of the row of five payphones in the main lobby, only one was unoccupied. Kathy snatched it up as quickly as she could. Dropping in the coins, she dialed in to check the messages on her answering machine back at the apartment.

She didn't expect any calls, but it gave her an excuse to get out of Samantha's room while the doctor broke the news that there was nothing medically that they could do to speed up the delivery. With the way Samantha's hormones had been raging lately, it was not going to be an easy conversation.

To Kathy's surprise, the robotic voice said, "You have one new message."

After the robot read off the phone number, which Kathy didn't immediately recognize, Michael's voice was in her ear.

"Hey, Kathy. It's Michael. Um…I was hoping to reach you. I just wanted to apologize, again, for overstepping last night. It blurred lines, but I was just happy to see you and…yeah." He let out a deep breath. "Anyway. I just want to be friends, if that's okay with you. Give me a call so we can talk. All right? Okay. Bye."

When the robotic voice came around again, Kathy hit the prompt that offered her to listen to the message again. Like the first time, it was preceded by the incoming telephone number and Kathy recited it to herself over and over.

Hanging up the phone, she flipped the switch for her change, then fed the coins in again. She had to add a few more to make the call. Still reciting the phone number, she dialed it and listened to it ring as her heart pounded in her chest.

"Hello?" Michael said when he picked up the phone.

"Hey, it's me. Kathy."

"Oh hi!" His voice picked up at that. "I called you, but I got your machine."

"I know. I just listened to your message."

"So, I'm assuming by your callback that you want to talk too?" he asked. "Do you want me to come over?"

"I'm actually not at the apartment—home." She had to start referring to her apartment as "home," otherwise she would never see it that way. "I'm calling from the hospital. Hamot. Samantha's in labor."

"Oh wow. That's exciting."

"Turns out exciting is also kind of boring." She laughed lightly. "The doctor said it's going to be a while, so it looks like we'll be here for most of the night."

"That's tough. How's Samantha doing?"

"Fine, considering. Her attitude needs an adjustment, but that's to be expected, I guess. She's just frustrated that things aren't happening on her timeline. You know how she loves to plan."

"You've mentioned it before."

That was another thing in Michael's favor. He and Kathy had history. He knew her family. They were all friendly with each other. He knew her life and parts of her past. It wasn't like starting over with a stranger, which was a refreshing thought. They had history. *Good* history.

"Yeah," she murmured.

"Well, I still want to talk to you," he said. "It sounds like you're going to have some downtime, so would it be okay if I met you there so we could talk?"

"And do what? Talk in the waiting room?" She made a face, then noticed the guy in the next booth over raising his eyebrow at her. She turned away, casually fingering the metal cord.

"I mean, we could..."

"No, there are too many people," she said. "It's too public of a place to have such a personal conversation. I want both of us to feel comfortable enough to be honest."

"We could go to dinner," he suggested. "There are some

decent restaurants not too far from Hamot."

"Hmm. Maybe."

"You don't seem to like that idea."

"It's just that I want to be nearby in case something happens with Samantha."

"She's not dying, Kathy."

"Right, but it's my first niece or nephew. Her first baby. And I'm her only sister—her only family, really. Well, besides Steven."

"Okay," Michael said with a sigh. Kathy could tell he was getting frustrated. "So where do you suggest we go?"

"Um…" She tapped her finger against the metal shelving below the phone that held the phone book. "I guess you can come here. We'll just have to find a private area in the cafeteria or something."

"Perfect, I can be there in about half an hour."

Kathy thought for a moment. That would give her time to go back up to Samantha's room, check in on her, and maybe even get her advice before talking to Michael.

"Sounds good," she finally said. "I'll see you then."

On her way back up to Samantha's room, she passed by the nursery. With evening approaching, many of the babies had already been returned for the night.

Kathy stopped and looked out at them. They were all so tiny. So young, with their whole lives ahead of them. She imagined that some would be doctors, lawyers, police officers, teachers.

Others would simply be mothers or friends or maybe even aunties, like her.

She couldn't help but wonder how many of them would be disappointed with their lives in some way. Maybe they'd regret not going after a promotion or not going to college or not settling down and having kids sooner.

Just like Kathy sometimes felt.

Out of the two of them, Samantha was the responsible one. The one who always had a plan and stuck to that plan. Kathy was the opposite of that. Not only in the way she viewed the world, but also sometimes as a conscious choice to be different from her sister. She was her own person, and she was determined to prove that by doing things differently than Samantha.

But here she was, about to become an aunt, and she couldn't help but notice how far apart her and Samantha's lives were. Her sister had a great, professional job that she enjoyed. She was married. She was about to become a mother.

Kathy, on the other hand, still wasn't sure what her passion in life was, as far as her career went. She so far couldn't make a relationship work, and was even becoming a caricature of the person she didn't want to be. What type of person dated their ex's best friend?

But the thought that weighed on her the most was the very real possibility that she would never feel settled enough to have her own children. Because for all of her struggles in life, there was one moral she was determined to keep: she was not going to bring a child into the world until she could properly support him or her. No child deserved to be neglected by a parent.

Not like she had been.

CHAPTER 16

Dennis paced the creaky floorboards of one the spare bedrooms in his parents' house. He had borrowed one of their old rotary phones, which he had plugged into the jack behind the dresser. The phone sat on the top of the dresser, right beside his bag of clothes.

What was holding him off from making the call was the fact that he was wrestling with himself over how deep he wanted to get into this. If he started making phone calls to other people, he would be crossing a line almost to the point of no return. As of now, the only ones he had really brought into his concern were his parents. But he had exhausted that source, especially now that they believed he had a crush on Kathy.

Let them think that, he thought to himself. *It's safer for them that way.*

As he paced the room, he glanced down at *The Art of Magic* that lay on his perfectly-made bed. Something he had picked up from the Navy. Always leave a room tidier than it was when you entered it.

The ancient tome—the *magical* tome, he now knew—stared at him, as if daring him to take the next step. He thought about his parents, oblivious to the powers these women had. The sisters who lived right across the street from them, who likely knew secrets about this very house. The ones his parents had invited over for dinner as if they were harmless.

Because Dennis's parents believed they were harmless. And that put them in danger.

If his parents were so blind to what these women—these *witches*—were, then who else was being fooled by it? How many other people were in danger because of their proximity to them? Steven possibly was even a victim, unless he was now one of them. Or maybe they had brainwashed him into sticking with them, so that he wouldn't blow their secret. Maybe he had a twisted loyalty to them out of fear.

It had to stop.

Dennis picked up the phone and began dialing. If he didn't stand up to them, who else was going to?

"Hamot Medical Center, how may I help you?" a cheery woman asked on the other end.

Dennis cleared his voice, then recited the line he had been practicing. "Hi, I'm calling from the road. My sister said she's in labor. I'm trying to hurry to get to her before the visiting hours end—I'm driving up from Pittsburgh and stopped at a pitstop to call you so I could make sure I made it in time. Could you tell me what room she's in?"

"When you arrive, one of the receptionists in the main lobby should be able to assist you." She sounded as if she were about to end the conversation, so he hurried to add his final push.

"It's just that, I'm running late and I don't want to waste time asking at the desk when I get there," he said, trying to play it cool. His heart was pounding in his chest, and he worried that his parents might overhear his blatant lies. "I'd hate to miss the visiting hours over something as trivial as protocol."

"You will have plenty of time," the woman assured him. "Our visiting hours aren't always strict, depending on the reason your relative is in the hospital."

"My sister," he said. "And that's good. But is it too much trouble to just tell me her room number? While I already have you on the phone?"

The woman sighed on the other end. Dennis could hear the tapping of a computer keyboard through the phone.

"What's your sister's name?" she asked.

"Samantha Harper."

CHAPTER 17

Samantha squeezed her husband's hand as she felt another contraction come. Sweat broke out all over her body as the pain kicked in. Then, almost as quickly as it came on, it passed.

She lay back in the bed and took in some deep breaths with her eyes closed. When she opened them again, she nearly spilled the cup of water that Steven had outstretched toward her. She snatched it from him and took a sip.

"Jeez, you almost dumped the damn thing all over me."

"Sorry." He reached for the empty cup, but she swatted his arm away and set it on the overhang table herself.

"I don't need you doting on me," she snapped. "I thought we talked about you hovering over me like a helicopter?"

"I was just trying help."

"Trust me, you've done enough. How do you think I got like this?" Samantha adjusted herself on the bed, doing her best to get comfortable, which was an impossible chore. No matter how she turned or twisted, she couldn't find a spot that felt right.

Steven sat in the chair and crossed his arms. He glanced up at the TV, which was playing a rerun of *Roseanne*. The sound was down so low that they could barely hear it and Samantha knew he was doing everything to avoid eye contact with her.

Or rather, he was doing everything to avoid snapping at her himself. She knew she was being mean to him—downright rude, actually—but it wasn't like she could help it much. Her body was in flux, hormones rushing through her, bringing intense anger and then, what was following now, sadness.

"I'm sorry," she croaked as the tears began to flow. "I'm being a bitch to you and you're only trying to help."

Steven's face immediately turned to concern and he pulled his chair closer to her and took her hand. "Hey, no. It's okay. Honey, don't cry." He reached up and wiped a tear away from her cheek.

"You probably feel so helpless, just sitting there and waiting for something to happen." She sniffled and patted his hand with her free one. "You're going to be a great dad."

"And you're going to be a great mom," he said.

At that, Samantha wailed even louder. She pulled away from him and squeezed her eyes shut as she cried.

"What's the matter?" he asked.

"I have no one!" she blurted. "Of course there's you, and Kathy, but otherwise there's no one here for me! I barely have any family." Her shoulders shook as she sobbed.

Steven stood and wrapped his wife in a hug. He leaned down and kissed the top of her head. "You have me and Kathy, like you said. We're not going anywhere."

"But my mother can't be here. She's missed everything, Steven! Basically our whole lives. And then our wedding and now this. I know she would've loved to see us grow up—to be here for the birth of her first grandchild." She shrugged. "But now she won't even get to meet them."

There was nothing that Steven could say that would relieve the pain of losing a parent, so he just squeezed her tighter as she cried.

Samantha patted his arm and pulled away from him. She reached toward the tissue box and Steven handed it to her. She pulled one out and blew her nose, then immediately reached for another to wipe her eyes.

"I'm a complete wreck," she said with a sad chuckle.

"I think you're beautiful," he said. "I know how hard it is for you to be so strong all the time. I wish you would realize that you don't always have to be. Not with me, at least."

She patted his arm and smiled at him through her tears. "Thank you, honey." Another chuckle. "Gosh, when I really get down to thinking about it, I even sometimes miss my father in times like these."

"Why shouldn't you?"

"Because he abandoned us!"

"Well, yeah. But he also raised you. On his own. After his wife died. Can't you offer him just a little bit of sympathy?"

Samantha sighed. She knew that she was often too hard on her father, but she still didn't understand how he could just disappear without a trace and never reach out to them. That line about going on a soul searching trip seemed so believable at the time. Maybe who she was really mad at was herself for falling for it.

"If he came back here right now and apologized, would you be able to forgive him?" he asked.

Samantha thought about it for a moment and then shrugged. "I don't know. And the worst part is, that's never going to happen. I just need to move on—I *have* moved on. But now I need to fill the roles of both my parents. For Kathy. For this baby. Don't you see? I have to be strong, because no one else is going to be strong for me."

Steven wanted to tell her that he would be her strength. That he would protect her. But there was only so much he could protect her from. He couldn't fight the demons—literal demons—she faced. He couldn't go back and fix what had happened to her parents. All he could do was be there for her in the moment.

"Hey," Kathy said in a chipper voice when she walked in.

She stopped and looked between the both of them. "Sorry. Did I interrupt something?"

Samantha pulled away from her husband. "No, we were just—"

Steven got to his feet and said, "I'm going to get something to drink."

CHAPTER 18

"rie Police Department, if this is an emergency, please call 9-1-1," a woman's voice said on the other end.

"No, I'm actually wondering if I can speak to one of your detectives," Dennis said. He twirled the phone cord around his finger as he talked. This was going way above and beyond. He was already nervous about bringing more people into his theory about his parents' neighbors, but law enforcement? That was borderline crazy.

"Is this about an ongoing investigation?"

"No, a closed case," he said. "I'm looking for Detective Janet O'Leary."

"Can I ask what this is pertaining?"

"I'd rather speak to Detective O'Leary personally."

The woman sighed audibly, wanting him to notice her annoyance. "Let me see if she's in. Please hold."

Classical music began playing in Dennis's ear as he waited. He paced the room, counting his steps until he crossed that one squeaky floorboard again and again. He had to adjust the way he turned so he didn't get the phone cord too twisted.

Finally, after several minutes on hold, another woman's voice picked up. "This is Detective O'Leary. What can I do for you?"

"Hi," Dennis said, surprised at her abrupt entrance to the conversation. Suddenly, the lines he had been practicing in his head disappeared. "Um, my parents live in the house of the Halloween murders from last year—as in Halloween, uh, 1988, I guess."

"That case has been closed."

"Yes, but I just had some additional questions about what happened here."

"All information has been released to the media," she said. "Your parents, specifically, have been notified as much as they need to know regarding the events that took place in that house prior to their ownership."

"Right, but I was hoping I could talk to you personally about—"

"Are you a part of the media? Is this a part of some follow-up story you're doing or something?"

"No, I'm not affiliated with the media in any way," he said.

"I'm just…I have some concerns. About the neighbors."

"Then I suggest you discuss this with the neighbors before you call the police, sir."

"Not all the neighbors," he said. "Just the ones who live across the street."

O'Leary was quiet.

"Hello?" he asked.

"The Walkers? Or rather, the Harper/Walker house?"

"The sisters?" Dennis wasn't sure where the Walker name fit in—maybe it was Samantha's maiden name—but he noticed that he seemed to finally have O'Leary's attention.

"Yeah, them. What about them concerns you?"

"I'm just curious as to their involvement of what went on that night," he said, then added a lie, "I've already talked to a few other people who were there that night—a couple of the hostages too."

"Oh, so you've already talked to the boyfriend?" she asked.

Boyfriend? Did she mean Steven? Or a boyfriend of Kathy's?

"Yes, I did," he said without missing a beat.

"So what do you want from me?"

"I'd rather discuss this in person, if you don't mind."

O'Leary sighed. "I'm kind of waiting out a witness right now, so I guess I have some time. If you wanted to stop by here now, we could—"

"Actually, could you meet me at the Hamot Medical

Center?" he asked. "I'm going up there in a minute to visit a friend, but I don't want to put this off any longer."

She sighed again. "I'm not meeting you in someone's hospital room."

"No, of course not," he said. "Why don't we meet in the cafeteria? It should be quiet there, with the late hour and all."

There was a long pause on the other end, then O'Leary said, "What the hell? Fine. Give me an hour or so. I'll be the one with the badge."

CHAPTER 19

What's his problem?" Kathy asked as she sat in the chair Steven had just vacated.

Samantha waved it off. "It's nothing."

"Did you tell him that this kid is likely to be a..." she lowered her voice, "...*witch*?"

"No, I didn't. That's not what we were talking about."

"Are you going to? Because you should."

"No, I'm not. Not now, at least."

"Sam, as the baby's father, he has a right to know."

"And what am I supposed to do at this point? Not only will I disappoint him by telling him about the baby's magic, making Steven feel even more isolated, but I'm also going to tell him that I lied to him for almost a year now. It'll break his heart."

Kathy bit her tongue, fighting the urge to say, "I told you so." Instead, she muttered, "You kind of dug yourself into a hole here."

"Do you think I can just say, 'Oh, by the way, this kid's a witch just like me. Sorry!'" Samantha shook her head. "I can't do that. It would only lead to Steven resenting me—and the baby—and I'm not putting that on our marriage, or in this baby's life. We're going to have a child. We need to think about their feelings before our own."

"And what do you think is going to happen when that baby starts showing signs of magic? Who's feelings will be important then?"

"We have a long time before that happens. It probably won't be until they're thirteen or fourteen, at least."

"That's not the point, Sam. Sooner or later, the truth is going to come out. The longer you wait, the harder it's going to be for you, your husband, *and* your child."

"I know that! But this whole thing has snowballed into something bigger than it should've and I can't turn back time. I'm not the one with the time specialty."

Kathy didn't point out that even though she had the time specialty, even she couldn't turn back time. "So what's your plan, then?"

"I'll just keep quiet about it until the baby is old enough to show signs of magic and then act surprised when it happens."

The young witch sat back in her chair and crossed her arms.

"And you think that's the best way to handle this?"

"Yes."

"So you're going to lie to your family for the rest of your life?"

Samantha rolled her eyes. "Oh please. Don't sit there and lecture me like you're any better. Or should we take a look at your track record with relationships? How's Jeremy, by the way? Oh, that's right, you're too busy sleeping with his best friend!"

The blow hit Kathy harder than she expected. She knew Samantha's words were fueled by her mood swings, but those words wouldn't have come out if there wasn't some kernel of truth to them. If Samantha hadn't already been thinking them in her right mind.

Instead, Kathy turned her attention to the TV. She wanted Samantha's words—some of the worst they'd ever exchanged as sisters—to linger in the room. She wanted Samantha to hear them over and over again in her own head. She wanted her sister to regret them.

Steven returned, carrying a bottle of 7Up. "Hey."

Samantha gave him a small smile. "Hey."

Kathy rose to her feet. "You can have your chair back, Steven. I'm meeting someone downstairs."

Without even a glance in her sister's direction, she walked out of the room.

CHAPTER 20

Dennis fumed with anger as he walked down 1st Street. It was late and the crickets sounded off in a nighttime symphony. Despite the fairly warm weather, not single person was out as he passed by the ranch-style houses. Apparently temperatures in the mid-fifties and -sixties was too cold for Louisianans.

This was not the way Dennis had expected his evening to go. He thought he was going to spend a relaxing night in with Tammy—maybe even get lucky—but instead she started an argument. All he was trying to do was say something sweet to her and she went and blew it all out of proportion.

Women.

Dennis squinted as a slow-moving car blinded him as they

drove by with high-beams on. On the outskirts of New Orleans and this close to the Naval base, there was a mix of Navy wives and the runoffs from the city. He noticed it in the houses he walked by. Some had perfectly manicured lawns with bountiful flower beds, while others had chipped paint, cracked driveways, and broken down cars sitting in front of the garage.

Why did Tammy choose to live in such filth?

What had started the argument had been Dennis's thinly veiled promise to marry her. Right after he graduated from the Naval Academy, he was stationed in New Orleans and met Tammy at a charity downtown. They hit it off right away and began seeing each other, even through his frequent trips at sea.

Now that he had some time with her again, he asked if she would make him an honest man. She said she would, but asked when it would be, which started the argument that led him to walking down a ratchet street at ten o'clock at night.

He came to the corner with Concession Street and turned right. The brush was overgrown and the houses closer to Highway 23 looked more tired than the ones hidden away from the main artery.

If Tammy were to marry him, he would move her out of this squalor as soon as he could. Even living on base would be better than this.

Tammy wanted to know the exact date that Dennis was going to make a lifelong commitment to her. She wanted to know when he was going to come through on his promise to marry her. As if he had his whole life planned out. Wasn't a promise to someday marry her enough? He had just joined the Navy, why was she so quick to have him leave his career already?

Clearly, she didn't like that answer and accused him of stringing her along, using her for a place to stay when he was back on base. She said that whenever he came back around, he moved right in and played house.

Before he left, he told her he was going to spare her one night of having to put up with him and stormed out. He had every intention of going back to base and staying there. But his feet took him elsewhere.

It was actually what he needed, though. Now that he was closing the distance back to Tammy's house, he could tell that he was already starting to calm down. His shoulders weren't as tense, his jaw had stopped clenching, and he was getting tired again. The anger was slowly washing away from him.

Dennis made it back to Tammy's place on Stockfleth Street and let himself in the front door. From the living room, he heard her talking, so he held off on calling out her name. Instead, he pulled off his sweatshirt and hung it on the hook behind the door and made his way down the hallway into the kitchen.

Tammy was probably on the phone with her mother or sister, complaining about him. If he was quiet enough and he lingered out of sight, he might be able to catch some of what she was saying about him.

Maybe she had come around too. Or maybe what she said

would determine if he ever came back to her again.

But as Dennis listened, he soon realized that she wasn't talking to anyone in particular, but chanting out loud to herself.

Hear my inner heart's desire,
Make the call of my love stronger.

Over and over again, she repeated the couplet. Dennis peered around the corner and saw Tammy sitting on the floor. In front of her lay an ornate cloth with a brass bowl resting in the center and two candles lit beside it. As she chanted, she waved her hands over the bowl and had her eyes closed.

"What the hell is this?" he blurted.

Tammy's eyes snapped open and she turned to look at Dennis. "Honey! You're home already!"

"What are you doing?"

She forced a smile as she got to her feet. "Oh, it's just a silly thing my girlfriends and I do sometimes. We, uh, write a letter to whoever we're angry with, burn it in a bowl, and say some goofy words over it. It's just for fun."

Dennis wasn't convinced. "Sounded more direct than just goofy words."

"It's nothing." She stepped close to him and tried to wrap her arms around him. "How was your walk? Feel better?"

He pushed her away. "I don't want you casting any spells on me, Tammy." Immediately his thoughts went back to Maggie in

Annapolis. He had narrowly escaped danger from her, and from an investigation into him for her death. He didn't want to go through the same thing again with Tammy.

"Is that how we got together?" he asked her. "With your voodoo?"

"It's not voodoo," she said. "And no, I didn't cast any spell on you."

"Then what the hell is that?" He pointed at the altar behind her.

"It's a time-honored tradition passed down in my family."

"So you're a liar."

She crossed her arms and took a step back. "Excuse me?"

"You just told me that it was something silly you did with your girlfriends."

Tammy opened her mouth to respond, but stopped when she realized she was caught.

"Were you ever planning on telling me what you're into?"

She set her jaw and stared at him, wordlessly.

Dennis turned and shook his head. "You know what? I'm done. I can't be with you if I can't trust you."

This time will be different, he told himself. *This time I'll just walk away and leave her be.*

He started toward the door, but seemed to hit an invisible wall before he could round the corner down the hall that led to the front door.

"What's wrong?" Tammy took a step toward him and

Dennis felt the wall move away.

Ignoring her, he tried to leave, but again felt the wall only a step further than he had before. As he grew frustrated, he felt a magnetic pull in Tammy's direction that he couldn't fight.

"What the hell's going on?" he demanded.

Her eyes were wide. "I must've messed up the spell somehow."

"So it was a spell!" Dennis couldn't fight the force pushing him toward her.

"It must've been when you interrupted it," she murmured, feeling herself pulled toward him too.

As Dennis passed by the kitchen counter, he grabbed for whatever he could manage. His fingers found purchase on the block of knives. He barely was able to grab ahold of one on his way to Tammy.

"Dennis, what are you doing?" she asked in a panic. She grabbed for the doorframe and tried to break the magnetic force herself.

Meanwhile, Dennis gave in, pointing the knife in her direction as his anger blinded him.

Magically, the two were drawn together with a sudden impact. Dennis held the knife low and felt it pierce into Tammy's stomach when her spell took full effect.

She gasped as the knife penetrated her.

"This is what you wanted, Tammy," Dennis taunted her. "This is the spell you cast. You did this to yourself."

Even as she struggled to hold on to life, her magic remained in effect. Dennis half wondered if he was going to be stuck against a dead woman for the rest of his life. But as she took her final breath, her magic wore off and Dennis was finally able to pull himself away from her.

As Tammy collapsed to the floor, he looked down at her and said, "That's what you get for playing me, witch."

CHAPTER 21

Dennis entered the hospital and looked around for the directional signs to follow. A woman walked in behind him and went right to the front receptionist, so he stepped out of her way as he looked around.

"Yes, I'm here to see my friend—or rather, my friend's sister," the woman told the receptionist at the desk only a few feet away from Dennis. "Samantha Harper. She's having a baby. What room is she in?"

Dennis's ears perked up and he watched the interaction. Could he really be so lucky?

"I'm sorry, ma'am," the receptionist said, "but unless the patient has informed you of the room themselves, I can't divulge that information."

"You don't understand," the woman said. "My friend and I go way back. Like, to middle school even. It's totally okay."

The receptionist held firm and shook her head. "I'm sorry."

"But can't you call up to her room and ask for permission or something?"

With a sigh, the receptionist said, "I suppose I could make the exception. Why don't you take a seat in the waiting area while I make the call? It may take some time, though."

The woman walked off to the cluster of seats and found one in the corner by herself. Dennis knew what room Samantha was in—*Why didn't this woman just say she was a relative?* he wondered—but decided to feel her out for additional information. If she knew the sisters, then she might have some other things to share about some of their *oddities*.

Dennis chose a seat several spots over from the woman and waited before he began talking. He needed to make sure she didn't view him as a threat. He leaned back, resting his arm along the back of the empty seat beside him and glanced in her direction.

She was checking her makeup in a compact mirror she had pulled from her purse. She sensed his eyes on her and looked over and smiled.

He returned the smile and said, "Just waiting on a buddy of mine. He's just having a minor procedure, but needed someone to drive him. Who are you here for?"

The woman packed up her mirror and turned her body in

his direction. "Oh, my friend's sister is having a baby. I thought I would be nice and pop in to say hello, but the woman at the desk is being difficult."

"That's nice that you wanted to say hi."

"Yeah," she said with a sigh. "It's not going to mean anything to her. Samantha isn't really a huge fan of mine."

"How come?"

"Oh," the woman waved off the comment with a limp wrist. "She thinks I'm kind of a mess because I like to have fun. Luckily her sister *also* knows how to have fun. She's been my bestie since, like, sixth grade."

"Wow, that's a long time."

"Yeah. Kathy and I have had a lot of fun. Although Samantha is starting to wear off on her. She thinks she needs to become an adult and be boring and all that. I mean, as long as you have a job and pay your bills, what difference does it make if you go out on the weekends?"

Dennis flash a smile at her. "True."

"I'm Trisha, by the way." She reached out her hand.

He shook it. "Dennis."

"Nice to meet you."

"Right back at you." He flashed another grin. "You must be really close to your friend if you're here on a Saturday night instead of hitting the bars."

"Gotta have my wingwoman."

"I'd say you're doing just fine without her."

Trisha threw her head back and laughed. "Okay, so maybe we should switch that. It's more like I'm *her* wingwoman."

"Is that her sister rubbing off on her again?"

"You could say that. Kathy just came off a long relationship and I've been trying to get her back out there, but she seems resistant."

"How long was she dating him?"

"Well, they were on and off for a couple years, then they were officially *off* for about a year, but they got back together at her sister's wedding."

"Stealing her thunder? Wow. Bold move."

Trisha beamed with pride. "That's my girl. Anyway, they just broke up at the beginning of the summer, so she's been kind of mopey since."

"But they were broken up for a year, so clearly she moved on a bit."

"Yeah, she had another boyfriend in there, but they obviously broke up."

"Why obviously?" Dennis tried to do the math in his head. Was the on-and-off boyfriend the one who was held hostage or was that the in-between boyfriend?

"I'm not sure of all the details, but I guess Kathy's neighbors had this party that was apparently this cover for some nasty things going on in their basement."

"What kind of nasty things?"

"Like I said, I'm not sure about the details. All I know is that the police were involved and there was a whole investigation and it's the first party I was glad I *wasn't* invited to."

Bingo, he thought. *We have a winner.* "Wow. So did this boyfriend see what was in the basement or something?"

Trisha shrugged. "I don't know. Kathy didn't really tell me much, just said that Milo was pretty messed up from it and that he's the one who broke it off."

"Yeah, I guess that could make any guy question things. Do you know if Milo ever got himself straightened out?"

Trisha shook her head. "I don't know. Kathy stopped talking about him. We used to see him at the club all the time, but after they broke up he stopped coming. I wonder if he moved away, but I guess he had a nice job with the city, so I wouldn't think he'd give that up easily."

"What did he do at the city?"

She rolled her eyes and waved her limp hand again. "I don't know. Something with trees and parks or something."

"Public Works?"

"Maybe. That sounds familiar. Why do you ask?"

"Just curious," he said. "But I do have a tree outside my house that needs to come down. It's dead and hanging over the house. Anyway, I have been meaning to call the city to ask them if they can take it down for me and maybe plant a new one while they're at it. It would really save me a ton of money."

"Oh, yeah, that stuff's not cheap. Or so I've heard." She laughed. "I rent, so I don't have to take care of stuff like that."

"Yeah, I can certainly see the advantages of renting," he said. "Hey, would you happen to have Milo's number? I'd love to make a more personal connection so they can't shut me down at the city before I can even talk to someone."

Trisha turned to her purse and dug for her address book. "Ugh, don't you hate that? I work in customer service and sometimes I have to do that myself. It really sucks."

As she talked, she jotted down a number on a scrap piece of paper and handed it to him.

"I wouldn't mention my name when you talk to him," she said. "That would probably remind him of Kathy and what happened and I'd hate to bring up old memories."

Dennis looked down at the number. "Wouldn't want to do that."

CHAPTER 22

Kathy cradled a cup of coffee between her hands as she waited for Michael to walk through the doors of the hospital cafeteria. She knew she had a bit of time still, but she just needed a break from Samantha for a while. Mood swings were not new for her sister—at least, not since the pregnancy hormones really got raving—but rarely was she as nasty as she had just been upstairs.

Kathy's foot shook beneath the table as she thought it over. Even though Samantha's comment was uncalled for, was it also a wake-up call? When Kathy had broken up with Jeremy, it was because she was getting her life together when he seemed to be just getting by.

And she *had* been getting her life together. She still enjoyed working with Dr. Newberg and the rest of his staff. She was living on her own for the very first time. And she was in the process of saving to buy her own car—not that public transit bothered her too much. She enjoyed people watching.

But jumping into bed—whether they actually did anything or not—with Michael was a sign that she hadn't grown as much as she thought she had. If she truly was going to grow as a person, she needed to be on her own for a while longer. Maybe she shouldn't be seeking guys out at all. Maybe she should just wait until she stumbled on the one who fit so perfectly into her life.

That's what Samantha had done. When she first met Steven, she was driven by her goal to keep the house and keep things normal for the sisters. She wasn't looking to date. And, as far as Kathy knew, Samantha had made it clear to Steven that taking care of herself came before their relationship. He loved her enough to support her, instead of giving her an ultimatum. If Samantha could do it, why couldn't Kathy?

The problem was, she liked Michael. How much, exactly, she wasn't sure.

Kathy's eyes flickered up when someone entered the cafeteria. It was getting late so there weren't too many people coming and going, despite the dinner hour. Apparently more people wanted to seek outside options for dinner while they visited people in the hospital. Kathy was just as grateful for the quiet.

But the person who entered caught her completely by surprise.

"Kathy?" Trisha shouted across the room as she spotted her friend. She raised her arms up and danced as she stepped to Kathy's table.

Kathy couldn't help but smile. Trisha truly didn't care what other people thought of her. She was a free spirit, which Kathy sometimes identified with, although not lately.

"Hey! What are you doing here?" Kathy asked.

"I wanted to visit your sister, but the receptionist is taking her time getting me her room number." Trisha took a seat across from her friend. She slipped her purse off her shoulder and draped it over the back of the chair. "I think she's stalling until visiting hours are over. I did meet this cute guy in the lobby, though."

"Of course you did. Anyway, Sam's in Room 348. Be warned, though. She's in rare form—and not in a good way."

Trisha made a face. "Is she being a bitch?"

Kathy chuckled. "You could say that."

"Is that why you're hiding out down here?"

"No, I'm actually meeting Michael here."

"Oh! Whatever happened last night? You just disappeared on me. I saw him come in, though, so I figured you were with him." She wiggled her eyebrows. "Did you take him upstairs?"

"Um…"

"Kathy!" Trisha squealed with delight and brought both

hands to her mouth to hide her wide grin. "Oh, you're just *living* life, girl!"

"It's not—nothing happened. I mean, not much. We did share a bed, but we did *not* sleep together in that way. At least, I don't think."

"If I know you, no matter how well you know a guy, you wouldn't sleep with anyone while you were drunk. You're more likely to pass out and snore."

"Hey!" Kathy smiled, grateful for her friend to bring some levity to the situation. "He did kiss me, though."

"Oh? Are you two an item now?"

"No. Maybe. I don't know. Is it bad if we are?"

Trisha leaned back in her chair and thought it over. "Hmm. Dating the ex's best friend? It's not great, but you and Jeremy have been broken up for so long."

Kathy shrugged. "Seven months."

"Then that's *plenty* of time! I mean, why are you going to hold off dating someone to spare the feelings of a guy who wasn't ever careful with yours?"

"True. It just seems…I don't know. Like we're doing something wrong, you know? Almost like an affair, even though I know it's not. I mean, we're both single and we're both fair game, but still."

"It's just because you two have history," Trisha said. "You were a part of their friend group—you saw Michael simply as a friend. And now that might be evolving into more. What's weird to you is change, not the guy."

"Maybe."

"Do you *want* to date him?"

Before Kathy could answer, she looked up and saw Michael walk in. She waved to him with a smile, then nudged Trisha under the table. Her friend took the hint and jumped to her feet.

As she slung her purse back over her shoulder, she mouthed to Kathy, "He's *fine!*" Over her shoulder, she called to Kathy, "I'm going to go check in with your sister. Call me if I don't see you!" On her way out the door, she waved to Michael.

"Did I interrupt something?" Michael asked as he approached.

Kathy got to her feet and greeted him with a hug. "Not at all. That was my friend Trisha."

"I remember. You invited her to the diner in Lawrence Park that one time. And I think she came with you to that college party when we all first met."

"Oh yeah! I forgot about that."

"Yeah." He looked toward the food counter and asked, "Anything good here?"

"I don't know," she said. "I'm not really hungry. I just got a coffee, but I don't think I've taken a sip of it yet so I can't tell you whether it's good or not."

"I'm guessing probably not," he said. "But have you really visited a hospital if you haven't had the twenty-five cent coffee?"

She smiled at his joke.

He pointed and said, "I'll be right back. I'm going to get my own cup of sludge."

Kathy retook her seat and tried to rehearse the upcoming conversation in her head, but no matter how she started it, nothing good ever seemed to come together. It was probably because she wasn't sure what she even wanted to say to him. She didn't know what she wanted.

Michael was back sooner than she expected. He took the seat Trisha had just vacated and shook a sugar packet in his hand. He dropped a couple small cups of creamer on the table beside his cup of coffee.

"I wanted to start right off the bat and apologize again for overstepping last night." He ripped open the packet of sugar and poured it into his coffee. "I've been remembering more as the day has gone on and I remember suggesting I spend the night. It wasn't right on my part, so I'm sorry."

Kathy remembered it differently, although in her version, things were awkward after the kiss and he wanted to drive home. She told him he needed to wait before she would let him drive. She distinctly remembered telling him he could stay at her apartment, but she couldn't remember her intention behind that invitation. After the kiss, did she *want* him to end up in her bed? Or was she simply looking out for his wellbeing by not letting him drive drunk?

"You don't need to apologize," she said. "Really. I mean, yes, jumping into bed together was certainly too fast—"

"For what it's worth, I don't think anything happened."

"Neither do I." She was happy that he thought the same thing she did. "But still. Whether or not anything *did* happen, we're adults. We can hit pause and slow down."

"Right." He finished doctoring his coffee and took his first sip. He made a face and pushed it aside. "So where do we go from here?"

"I think it's best if we just lay it all out on the table," she said. "As uncomfortable as that is for us."

He nodded. "I agree."

She smirked. "You just want me to go first."

"If you're offering."

She rolled her eyes with another grin. Being vulnerable wasn't easy. "Okay. Um…well, I was happy to see you, and to catch up. I haven't seen you since Jeremy and I broke up and I missed you."

"I missed you too," he said.

She noticed his hand was on the table. Was he offering it if she wanted to take it? She kept both of hers clutched around her coffee cup. The contents of it had long gone cold.

"Actually," he went on, "if I'm being honest, when you guys broke up, I was kind of bummed because I knew that meant that our friendship would end too, since I was Jeremy's friend first. But then I realized that—"

"That Jeremy can be a jerk sometimes?" she cut in. She was happy that this was the direction the conversation had taken.

Friendship. Michael was only interested in friendship. She could certainly handle that.

He laughed. "Yeah, exactly."

"You know I'm not telling you to choose him or me, right? You can be friends with me and Jeremy at the same time. The fact that Jeremy and I don't want to see each other anymore is our problem, not yours."

"I just don't know if Jeremy would agree."

She shrugged. "He needs to grow up and accept the fact that we each are only responsible for ourselves. So do what makes you happy. We can continue to be friends."

Michael sighed and studied his cup. "The problem is…I was kind of hoping that maybe you and I could be…*more* than friends."

And with that, Kathy's hope at an end to the discomfort between them fizzled.

CHAPTER 23

etective O'Leary walked into the hospital cafeteria like a woman in charge. She wore her police badge proudly on the belt of her gray pantsuit. She had a mass of curly hair that had been tamed by what Dennis could only assume was an endless amount of products.

Once she was through the door, she put her hands on her hips and looked around.

From a table in a corner, Dennis waved her over. He was careful not to draw too much attention. He had noticed Kathy sitting at a table with a man when he walked in. Luckily, she didn't know who he was so he was able to avoid her without detection.

"Are you Dennis Kors?" O'Leary stood behind the seat

across from him, one hand still on her hip.

"Yes, ma'am."

Under her breath, she muttered, "What do you know? You actually showed." Then she pointed to the counter and said, "I'm going to order a coffee before they close. I'll be right back."

Without waiting for a reply, she crossed the room to get her beverage.

In her absence, Dennis thought about the hole he was digging himself into. What did he really know about the women who lived across from his parents?

He knew they were witches.

But would Detective O'Leary take the book of spells as definitive proof that they were witches? He could always sneak back over and steal some of their potions that he had found, but that would be illegally obtaining evidence and could be easily thrown out in court—if it ever got to that point.

What was he accusing them of anyway? Being witches? Was there a law that said you couldn't be? Worse, if he failed in his attempt to take them down, would that just launch an attack against him—or his parents?

Based on what Dennis had seen from people who possessed supernatural powers, they felt as if they were above the law. Above morals and ethics. Better than everyone else. All because they had *abilities*. They needed to be stopped.

"For the record," O'Leary said when she returned with her coffee. Her voice startled him and he tried not to show it, but nothing got passed the trained interrogator. "Sorry," she muttered. "Scaring people is an old habit of mine."

Dennis shook his head. "You didn't scare me."

She hooked an eyebrow in disbelief. "Anyway, for the record, I can't officially disclose anything about the case. I don't care where you live or who you're related to. The case is closed. The victims involved—and their families—have all been notified already."

"I understand," he said. "I was just hoping to pick your brain on the sisters—" His eyes flickered over to where Kathy sat on the other side of the room with her back to him. "Samantha and Kathy. What did you make of them?"

O'Leary took a long sip of her coffee as she thought. It was black, Dennis noticed. This woman didn't mess around.

"Well, that was over a year ago, so I can't rely on my memory for specific examples for you," she started. "What I will say is this: after I interviewed the two of them, I had this weird vibe about them."

Dennis perked up, glad that someone else was saying the same thing he felt about them. "Weird vibe?"

"Yeah. Like they were hiding something."

"You think they were involved with what happened?"

She leaned back in her chair. "The evidence didn't point to that. Officially, they weren't involved."

"Right. But what do *you* think?" he pushed. When she remained quiet, he added, "Off the record."

"Off the record?"

He nodded.

She let out a deep breath. "I think they know more about what happened than they let on."

"So they lied to a police officer," he said. "Interfered with an investigation. Aren't those crimes?"

"Hey, I'm not trying to go after these women. The case is closed and nothing else has happened—to my knowledge—in their presence. So as far as I'm concerned, these women should be left alone to do what they want with their lives."

"But if you said they're hiding something—"

"What is it you really want to know?" She looked at him with raised eyebrows over the rim of her cup. "Does it have anything to do with you asking to meet me in the same place where one of the sisters just happens to be?"

He glanced over at Kathy again, then back to O'Leary.

The detective took another sip of her coffee, then asked, "Didn't think I noticed that, did you?"

"Call it a coincidence."

She raised her eyebrows in disbelief. "Mm-hmm."

"I heard the sisters were close to some of the hostages who were held in the basement."

"Who told you that?"

"So it's true?"

"They lived across the street," O'Leary said. "They were at a combination housewarming and Halloween party. It's not unusual for them to know some of the victims."

"I heard they were boyfriends to the sisters."

She chewed on her lip and shook her head. "Sounds like *you* know more about this case than you let on."

"My parents are a part of the neighborhood now too," he said. "They've talked to some people."

"So why don't you just keep asking the neighbors?"

"Because I'm asking you. Steven and Milo were there, weren't they?"

"And Harry."

That was a new name. Dennis didn't react to that, though. Not like he did when O'Leary came up behind him. This time, he was better prepared.

"Right," he said. "They were the survivors."

"And then the two who had been previously deceased." She glanced at her watch. "How much longer are we going to be? I have to get back to my witness before he falls asleep in my interrogation room."

"I think that's it," he said.

She rose to her feet. "Good, because this was a waste of my time. Next time you have trouble with your neighbors, just talk to them." She nodded to where Kathy was seated. "You don't seem to have any issue finding them. I don't think you need to involve the police." She turned and began to walk away.

"Detective O'Leary," Dennis called after her.

She turned and put one hand on her hip while she held her

coffee in the other. "Yeah?"

"Thank you for meeting me. And I hope you understand that I'm just trying to keep my parents safe."

CHAPTER 24

Samantha fidgeted with her hospital wristband. She couldn't stop thinking about the way she had snapped at Kathy and how she had rightfully stormed out. It was a time when everyone was trying to show Samantha their support and she was throwing it right back at them.

Even Kathy's friend Trisha had just come to visit her. Thankfully, it was a short visit, since that particular friend of Kathy's Samantha wasn't too fond of. But still, it was nice that she came. The part that stung, though, was Trisha admitting that Kathy was stewing down in the cafeteria, waiting for Michael so they could talk.

Was Samantha pushing Kathy into his arms before she had a chance to really think about what it was that she wanted?

Samantha had cruelly pointed out the poison that surrounded a potential union between Kathy and Michael, but she had said it in the heat of the moment after feeling backed into a corner about her own relationship.

Just because Kathy knew Michael as Jeremy's friend, didn't mean that a relationship between the two of them couldn't work out. Samantha just wanted her sister to think about it thoroughly first. More importantly, she wanted to be a part of that conversation—a confidante her sister felt she could turn to, no matter how much older they got or whether they lived together or apart.

Samantha feared her mood swings were tarnishing their sisterhood.

"Good evening, Mrs. Harper," a young man said when he entered the room. He had a clipboard with him, which he tucked under his arm as he stepped toward her with his hand extended. "I'm Dr. Mitchell, the anesthesiologist on staff here at Hamot. Dr. Mendon wanted me to go over the plan for painkillers with you."

She attempted to sit up straighter, but she didn't want to move too much. She had finally found a position that was relatively comfortable. Although, that was probably more to do with the fact that she hadn't had a contraction in a while.

"Yes, hi." She shook his hand, then motioned over to Steven, who had read her tone and had been sitting quietly by himself in a chair by the window. "This is my husband, Steven."

Dr. Mitchell shook his hand as well, then turned back to Samantha, clipboard and pen at the ready. "First of all, let me ask you this: are you interested in painkillers? Some women try to do the whole thing natural."

Samantha shook her head. "I'm not most women. Give me the drugs."

He laughed. "Okay. I'll mark that down for you. There's either women who don't want anything or those who want *everything.*"

"Give me everything," she said.

Dr. Mitchell tucked the clipboard under his arm again. "Well, what we normally do is give you a gradual dose—just through your IV, and then we'll increase as needed. However, I want to warn you that there will still be a lot of…discomfort."

Samantha locked eyes with him. Before she knew what she was really doing, she could feel the magic seeping out of her in his direction as she said, "Listen to me carefully. I don't want to feel anything when this baby comes out."

His eyes went blank, still locked with Samantha's. "I'll get you whatever you want."

"Samantha!" Steven barked, breaking both doctor and patient out of the magical trance.

Dr. Mitchell shook his head, clearly confused as to what just happened.

Steven cleared his throat and asked the doctor, "How far

along does she need to be before you start to administer the meds?"

The doctor rubbed his forehead as he tried to regain his train of thought. "Um…it depends on how far along you are and what level you're experiencing the pain."

"She's not in too much pain, really." Steven shot his wife a warning look, then turned back to Dr. Mitchell. "Her other doctor said that she isn't even halfway yet. I wouldn't want to start giving her anything until she's closer." He turned to Samantha. "Right, *dear*?"

She shrugged. "The pain is bearable for now."

"Good." Dr. Mitchell nodded absently, then seemed to just remember his clipboard. He flipped through a couple pages. "I'll—I'll go confer with Dr. Mendon and then I'll be back."

When the door shut closed behind him, Steven turned to Samantha and asked, "You were using your magic on him, weren't you? Persuasion?"

Samantha crossed her arms and glanced up at the TV.

"You can't do that, Sam!" he said. "Do you understand how dangerous that is? You need to trust these doctors to use their *own* minds to give you the best medical advice and use their best judgment. You can't manipulate that."

She took a deep breath and said, "I know."

"So promise me you're never going to do it again."

Chewing on the inside of her cheek, she kept her arms crossed and refused to look in his direction. "Fine."

There was silence, but Samantha could still feel her husband's eyes on her.

"Sam, what's going on with you?" Steven asked. "You're not acting like yourself lately—and you can't blame it all on the baby. All day it's been one thing after another. You're paranoid about the neighbor, then you're snapping at me. You clearly said something awful to your sister if *she's* even avoiding you. And now you go and use your powers on a doctor? This isn't you. What's up?"

Her shoulders dropped and she finally looked at him. Above all else, she saw in him someone she could trust with the truth. Hadn't he proved again and again that he was always going to be around to support her, no matter what?

"I'm scared," she admitted.

"About the baby?"

"About having the baby, about taking care of the baby, about raising the baby, about some evil force showing up and *hurting* the baby," she said. "And then there's me and you. Our relationship is certainly going to be different. You're not taking as much time off as I am. Am I going to resent you going to work while I'm stuck at home taking care of the baby while I'm also healing? Are we going to grow apart without even realizing it and end up getting divorced, which will only lead to this kid having a broken home? And then we're back to my fear of raising the baby!"

Steven pulled his chair to the side of her bed and took her

hands in his. "Honey, it's perfectly normal to be afraid of the unknown."

"This isn't the unknown. Things are going to change—and soon. That's very well known. It's just…it's all becoming very *real* to me."

"Look, I know you like to be in control of everything and it seems like your body and this baby are making decisions that you're not ready to make yet. But think of it this way: if every other mother can do it, so can you. You're not the first to worry about these things and you're certainly not going to be the last. You can handle this. *We* can handle this."

Samantha pulled one hand away from his to wipe at a tear forming in the corner of her eye. "I know all of that, but it would be a lot easier to manage if I had a mother here who has done it all before too." She shrugged. "And, at the risk of starting another fight with you, I think it's pretty obvious that I don't have a mother-daughter relationship with *your* mother, either. Having a role model who has been through this before isn't something that I have and it's not something that you can give me, as much as you want to."

Steven's face dropped as he accepted her words. "You're right. I can't bring your mother back. All I can offer you is my support. And I know Kathy would say the same thing. So don't push us away. We're only here to help."

"I know." She patted his hand. "And I love you for it."

He kissed her, then brushed her hair out of her face. "Just

think, after everything you've faced magically, I'd say that childbirth is far from the scariest of them all."

She smiled. "You'd be surprised!"

CHAPTER 25

After talking to Detective O'Leary, Dennis decided to take a seat in the main lobby. He wanted to be at the hospital to keep an eye on the sisters and the people in their lives. He had dodged a bullet with O'Leary and Kathy in the cafeteria. With the size of the space, he didn't think Kathy had overheard his conversation with the detective.

Still, he didn't want to linger in case Kathy somehow recognized him, so after his chat with O'Leary was done, he made his way back to the main lobby.

Trisha was gone by the time he got there, which was fine with him. He had her number in case he needed to grill her more, but he thought he had gotten as much out of her as he was going to get.

Just as he sat down in the lobby, he noticed a late-middle-aged couple walk in from the cold. The woman was dressed in a peacoat that covered her down to her knees. She had a scarf wrapped around her neck and black gloves, which she peeled off as soon as she entered the hospital. Her companion wore a black leather jacket, khakis, and sneakers. His fists were buried deep in his pockets and when he got inside, he rubbed them together to warm them.

The two of them had such a nervous energy about them that Dennis couldn't help but eye them curiously. He listened closely as they approached the receptionist.

"Hi, um, we're here for our first grandchild." The woman giggled. "Oh, that sounds so weird to say! I mean, do I *look* like a grandma?"

To Dennis, she did. But maybe it was the late hour or his faltering eyesight that wasn't doing her any favors.

"So you're family?" the receptionist asked.

"Oh yes," the woman said. "It's our son's baby."

"You'll probably want to search for his wife, Samantha Harper," the man cut in.

The receptionist tapped away at her computer and a moment later, she said, "Yes, I've got her here. Room 348. Take the elevators just around this corner to the third floor. When you get up there, take a right and you'll see the nurse's station. They'll be able to buzz you in. I'll let them know you're coming."

Interesting, Dennis thought to himself. *You have to be*

buzzed in. I wonder if they'll allow me to enter when the time's right.

"Okay, thank you." The man began to lead his wife toward the elevators.

Dennis watched as they pressed the call button. He considered for a second, and then sprung to his feet. He approached them just as the elevator doors opened and several people stepped out.

The woman smiled at him and then met his eyes, silently asking who was going to proceed onto the empty elevator first.

Dennis put his hand over the doors to hold it open, then motioned for the couple to enter with his other hand. "After you."

"Oh, thank you," the woman murmured. "Such a gentleman."

"What floor are you going to?" the man asked.

"The third floor," he said. "A friend of mine is having a baby."

"Oh, congratulations!" the woman cheered. "Our son is having his first baby."

The man pressed the button for the third floor, then turned to his wife. "Our son isn't the one in labor." He laughed. "It's his wife. You'll have to excuse my wife."

"I knew what she meant," Dennis said. "How exciting! How many other grandchildren do you have?"

"Oh, this is the first one," the woman said. "Our son's wife has insisted on keeping the gender a secret until birth, which is a little disappointing. I'm hoping for a little granddaughter. I've already bought several dresses and clothes that would be *perfect* for a baby girl!"

"But it could also be a boy," the man said. "We really just want the baby—and our daughter-in-law—to be healthy. That's what really matters."

"Yes, naturally," the woman said dismissively. "That was implied. But the *baby* is really why we're here."

Seems to be a case of "No one is good enough for my son," Dennis thought to himself. *Could work to my advantage.*

The elevator dinged just before the doors opened. Dennis followed the couple around the corner to a window and tapped the bell.

A nurse noticed them and pushed the window open. "Who are you here for?"

"Steven Harper," the woman said automatically, then added, "Baby Harper."

"Who's the mother?" the nurse asked.

"Oh, Samantha Harper," the woman said.

The nurse smiled. "Go right on in."

With the sound of a buzz, the doors leading to the maternity floor were unlocked and the three of them stepped through.

Dennis took a seat in the small waiting room on the maternity floor. He grabbed a forgotten newspaper from a nearby chair and raised it in front of him. He glanced over the top, making sure that Steven—or even Samantha—wouldn't walk by and recognize him. He would have to think about how he would spin it if he was discovered by them. For now, though, he was at least on the right floor. He could figure out his plan for the baby—the new *witch*—later.

The woman and her husband took a seat in the waiting room. As the woman sat, she let out an audible huff to announce her displeasure.

"It's only a few minutes," the man assured her. "Just while the doctor's checking in on her."

"Well, I'm just saying, it's bad enough that we couldn't get here sooner because you decided to spend today, of all days, driving by the house from *A Christmas Story* in Cleveland. And now we have to wait."

"It's five minutes," the man said. "She hasn't even had the baby yet."

The woman crossed her arms and huffed again.

"I'll get you some coffee," he muttered before rising and disappearing around the corner.

With her husband gone, Dennis slid over beside the woman and said, "So tell me about your daughter-in-law…"

CHAPTER 26

More than friends?" Kathy asked as she stared at Michael's pleading eyes across the table. "Oh…"

"It's just that, we've always gotten along great. And we hit it off so well last night when we ran into each other. And then there was the kiss and waking up this morning—"

"Yes, I remember," she said before he could finish. She didn't need to be reminded of her poor decisions the night before.

"You don't seem too keen on the idea."

Kathy rolled her neck, feeling it pop from the stress and the lack of sleep. All she wanted to do was flop in her bed and forget the world. "It's not that," she started.

"Then what is it?" Michael's broad shoulders seemed drooped inward.

She sighed. "If I'm being completely honest, I've been thinking about the same thing since last night. There's certainly chemistry between us. And I definitely felt something in that kiss."

"But…?"

"But I'm not sure how any type of romantic relationship between us would work."

"Is this about Jeremy?"

She ran her thumb along the rim of her styrofoam cup. "Of course it is. You and I have history because of Jeremy. Connections to other people because of my former relationship with him. All the people we used to hang out with at the diner, not to mention your family and mine."

"So you don't want to date me because of what other people might say? Kathy, that's—"

"It's not about what they're going to say. It's just that…" She sighed again, trying to think of the best way to articulate her feelings. Especially when she wasn't exactly sure how she felt to begin with. "Things between me and Jeremy didn't work out, okay? I've come to accept that, but that doesn't mean I want to put myself in an awkward situation."

"What kind of awkward situation do you mean?" Michael asked. "It's not like I'd expect you to hang out with him or anything. I just told you I need a break from him myself."

"A break, sure, but not a break-up."

He narrowed his eyes. "I hope you're not implying that Jeremy and I are—"

"No, of course not, but the fact remains that you two will probably continue to be friends, even after you take your break from him," she said. "And eventually it'll be more difficult *not* to include me—or him—in different things. Which means Jeremy and I will *have* to see each other."

"I'm still not following."

"Jeremy and I dated for a while. We broke up a couple different times and I kept going back, even though deep down I guess I sort of knew it wasn't going to work out. It's like there's this magnetism between me and him. Jeremy and I have chemistry too. And, while I'd never cheat on anyone, I don't want to lead you on if I start to develop feelings for Jeremy again simply because of proximity and nostalgia."

Michael shook his head. "That's not going to happen. You're overthinking it."

She raised her eyebrows because even she had to agree. Part of her sister was rubbing off on her.

"Like I said," he went on, "I need a break from him. But also, I need to grow up a little. That's really the main reason I'm getting my own place. I want to be my own person. And, sure, I'd love to be able to keep my friendship with Jeremy, but that depends more on Jeremy than anyone else. Jeremy's not Jeremy anymore. He needs to grow up too before I'd even consider continuing any kind of friendship with him."

That thought made Kathy sad because whatever her ex was going through, he was apparently doing it alone. But she had to remind herself that it wasn't her concern anymore. They had broken up for good this time. She couldn't keep running back to him. Especially not when she had a perfectly good man sitting across from her who wanted to be with her.

"You're right," she said. "Jeremy was going off the deep end when we broke up."

"Yeah."

"But Jeremy's not my only concern about us. What you and I have now is a good friendship. One that I really enjoy. I love being able to run into you at a bar and spend hours catching up as if no time has passed. If we start dating and it doesn't work out…" She shrugged. "Then what happens?"

Michael sucked in his bottom lip as he took a deep breath. "I mean, I would miss that too. But what if our relationship just grew into something even greater? What if our friendship is just our starting point?"

That was an endearing idea, but Kathy had had so many bad relationships that she wasn't sure if she believed it could be possible for a friendship to turn into a lifelong love. But wasn't that exactly what had happened with Samantha and Steven? Maybe there was hope.

"Maybe," she said as a yawn took over. Her tiredness was catching up to her, from the late night the night before to the late night tonight—and a long day of doing nothing but waiting. "Sorry," she told Michael. "You're not boring me. I was just up late."

He winked at her. "Get lucky, did you?"

"Hmm, that's yet to be decided." She reached for his hand and squeezed it. "Look, I know you came here to talk through things, but the truth of the matter is that I don't want to rush into anything. Nor do I want to shoot anything down immediately. This is all still so new." She checked her watch. "I mean, we just got reacquainted less than twenty-four hours ago! Let's sit on it before we jump into the next step."

He squeezed her hand back. "Fair enough."

She stood and pulled at his hand for him to stand too. "All I ask for is time to think things over. Besides, *I'm* here to be there for my sister, as difficult as she's been making that for me."

"No, I completely understand," he said. "Give me a call when you're ready to really talk. I'll be there for you."

"Thank you, Michael." She wrapped her arms around him and squeezed him tight. "I'm just trying to make sure we don't get hurt."

"I would never want to hurt you."

"I just don't think my son has fully thought through the commitment," Mary went on.

Once Dennis had opened up the can of worms that was talking about Mary's daughter-in-law, Samantha Harper, the woman just didn't seem to stop. Dennis had only caught her name when her husband, Marty, came back with her coffee and said, "Mary, give the man a break!"

She had quickly snapped back, "Oh, hush up, Marty," and continued to drone on about the things that "bothered" her about Samantha.

While some of those things had aligned with what Dennis had heard and what he himself was worried about—"Steven seems to be under her spell, the way he's so loyal to her" or "the mystery of her parents has never sat well with me" or "their house always has a very *distinct* odor and I'm not convinced it's from growing their own tea leaves"—others had been very petty—"she refuses to make the cheesy mashed potatoes because she says they're unhealthy, but they're my son's favorite" or "she's stuck in her ways" or simply "she just doesn't seem very friendly."

Throughout the conversation, Dennis had tried to keep a friendly smile the whole time. After all, he had started the discussion, which was really more of a one-sided conversation with the occasion "mm-hmm" and "oh yeah?" from Dennis. Still, he was grateful when a nurse in pink scrubs stepped into the waiting room and approached the Harpers.

"Are you Samantha Harper's family?" the nurse asked.

"Our son is married to her, yes," Mary said. "Has the baby arrived?"

The nurse shook her head. "Not yet. I'm afraid it's still going to be a while before he or she makes their arrival."

"They *still* haven't asked about the sex of the baby?" Mary asked.

"They've made it this far, dear, what's another hour or two?" Marty asked his wife.

"If you'd like to go in and see Mrs. Harper, I'm sure she'd appreciate that," the nurse said.

Not likely, Dennis thought to himself. As much as he didn't trust Samantha—or her sister—he couldn't help but feel a little bad for her for having to put up with such a pompous mother-in-law.

"Just a quick visit," the nurse added. "We'll want her to rest as much as she can before the baby really starts coming."

The Harpers rose to their feet.

"After we see her, though, we can stay here until the baby comes, right?" Marty asked. "Even if it's the middle of the night?"

The nurse smiled and nodded. "Of course. As long as it's okay with the parents."

Mary waved her hand as she walked by the nurse. "Oh, it'll be no trouble, I'm sure." Before she rounded the corner out of sight of the waiting room, she turned back and waved to Dennis. "It was nice chatting with you!"

He waved back politely and smiled. "My pleasure!"

After they were gone, he was the only one left in the waiting room. That fact made him uneasy. He could already feel the nurses eyeing him as they walked by. He didn't need to be drawing attention to himself. He had already successfully made it onto the maternity floor. He could do it again if he needed to. For now, he had other things to do.

Pulling the paper out of his pocket that Trisha had given him, he made his way back to the elevators. There was a row of payphones in the main lobby. It was nearly seven, but not too late for a phone call.

Maybe Milo would even be okay with meeting up sooner than later.

CHAPTER 28

Kathy stretched up on her toes to hug Michael again at the main doors into the hospital. Each time they embraced, it became more natural to slide in between his arms. It was both comforting and concerning to her.

Sure, she found solace in his presence, but what did it say about her that she could jump from one guy to another? It wasn't like she thought of herself as some kind of floozy, she genuinely made—or attempted to make—connections with the men she dated. But despite her best efforts, none of them had ever worked out. What made Michael different? Maybe she was the problem and not the guys who went out with her.

"Thanks for coming to see me," she said when they parted. "I'll call you later. Drive safe."

He squeezed her hand before pulling away. "Tell your sister congrats. When the baby comes, that is."

"I will." She waved and watched him walk out into the cold.

When he was finally out of eyesight, she turned and made her way back to the elevators. She hit the button for the third floor and waited, trying not to allow her thoughts to be caught up in Michael. She was here for her sister. For her first niece or nephew. Today wasn't about her.

Up at maternity, she told the nurse through the window who she was there to see and was buzzed in with a friendly smile and a wave. The nurse had been working earlier when Kathy came up and recognized her.

As she rounded the corner, she heard another nurse talking to someone in the waiting room.

"Of course," the nurse said. "As long as it's okay with the parents."

From behind, Kathy could see that it was Steven's parents the nurse was talking to.

"Oh, it'll be no trouble, I'm sure," Mary said with a wave. Her and Marty began to follow the nurse down the hall, but turned and waved to a man in the waiting room. "It was nice chatting with you!"

The man smirked and offered a quick wave. "My pleasure!"

Kathy pretended to be interested in the bulletin board on the wall. Her eyes kept flickering to the man, trying to figure out who he was. He was young, reasonably attractive, but a total and complete stranger. Where did Mary know him from and why was he in the maternity waiting room? There was no one else in there waiting with him.

The man pulled a piece of paper out of his pocket and quickly walked right by Kathy. By turning her back to him, she hid her face as much as she could without drawing attention to herself.

He walked right through the doors leading to the elevators and pressed the call button.

Did he come up here just to talk to Steven's parents? she wondered. *Why would they let him up if he didn't even know Samantha? She would've mentioned something if Steven's parents were bringing someone with them. Then again, knowing Mary...*

Kathy did her best to push the thought from her mind and made her way down the hall to her sister's room. Steven's parents were still lingering in the hall just outside her door.

"Hey, how are you guys?" she asked with a smile.

Marty immediately turned and gave Kathy a friendly hug, which was likely what prompted Mary to do the same.

"We're good, dear," Steven's mother said near Kathy's ear as they hugged. "The nurse said the doctor was checking on the baby, so we're just waiting out here for a few minutes."

Panic overcame Kathy. "She already had the baby!?"

Marty put his hand on her shoulder. "No, he's checking to see how *Samantha's* doing."

"Oh." She put a hand on her chest and relaxed. "I was afraid I missed it."

"So were we," Mary said in an irritated tone. She cast a side-eye glare at her husband.

"It's kind of my fault we're late," Marty admitted. "But we're here now."

Mary still looked annoyed and Kathy couldn't think of a good enough reason to leave—not to mention the fact that she *wanted* to see her sister because it had been a while since she had stormed out.

"So!" Kathy started abruptly. "I noticed you talking to someone in the waiting room. Was he a friend?"

"You didn't recognize him?" Mary asked. "He said he was an old friend of your sister's. Knew about you, too."

Kathy turned and glanced back at the waiting room. "Hmm. I didn't recognize him. But it could've been a friend from college."

"Maybe," Mary said. "He was asking about the both of you, how you're doing, what you've been up to. I got the impression that he's single, in case you're looking again."

The snub didn't go unnoticed, but Kathy just smiled politely and said, "Maybe if I remembered him I'd consider it. But I'm more worried about my sister and the baby."

The doctor emerged from the room and smiled at the three of them. "She's all yours."

"Thank you!" Kathy said as she marched into Samantha's room, grateful for the break from Steven's mother.

CHAPTER 29

The faux leather seat squeaked as Dennis and Milo settled in at opposite sides of the booth. To Dennis's surprise, Milo had agreed to meet with him right away, so Dennis suggested a diner right around the corner from the hospital on North Park Row. It was late, Dennis hadn't had dinner yet, and the casual atmosphere was hopefully enough to let Milo's guard down.

After they ordered, though, Milo wasted no time cutting to the chase.

"So what exactly do you want to know about Kathy?" he asked, resting his hands on the table. His fingers were intertwined together and Dennis wondered if that was to keep his hands still while he recalled any bad memories.

Dennis did his best to offer a friendly smile. "Nothing crazy, I promise you. Truthfully, I was curious about your relationship with her."

Milo stiffened as he sat up straighter in his seat. "What do you want with her?"

"I'm not stalking her," Dennis said. "I met her at work and I've been considering asking her out. I just want to make sure she's not, you know, crazy." He reached for the pie menu tucked behind the napkin holder and scanned it casually.

There was a pause. It took everything in Dennis to keep his body language relaxed. If he was quiet long enough, Milo would talk. They always did.

"Kathy's nice," Milo finally said. "She seemed a bit lost with her life when I was with her, but that was over a year ago. A lot could've changed since then."

Dennis put the menu back. "So there wasn't anything…*weird* about her that you noticed?"

"What exactly are you getting at?" Milo asked.

Dennis hung his head and sighed. "Okay, so there was this rumor at work that Kathy—" He shrugged. "—you know, that she dated more than one guy at a time. Was there anyone else when you were with her? Or any threat of one?"

He certainly didn't give a crap if she was a two-timing floozy, but from what he had learned so far, there was a third captive in the basement that night. Samantha's husband, Milo, and someone else. He needed to find out who that third captive was and he had a good idea it was someone who had been romantically tied with Kathy. According to Mary, Kathy was a flirt with multiple boyfriends.

Milo was quiet on the other side of the table.

The waitress came back and set their drinks in front of them. She was a young girl, probably working later than was legally possible. The owners must've been paying her under the table for the late shifts. "Your food will be right out, guys. Is there anything else I can get for you?"

"No thanks, sweetie," Dennis said. "You've been great so far."

She smiled at them and walked away.

Dennis took a look around the nearly empty diner, then leaned in across the table. "Okay, Milo, man-to-man: I just want to know if there was another guy in the picture. If there was, then she has a reputation and I don't want to get involved."

"There wasn't another guy."

"Huh?" He tucked a finger behind his ear and turned his head. "What was that?"

"I said there wasn't another guy."

"Sorry if I don't believe you, but your hesitation raises some doubts in my mind. Are you *sure* there wasn't anyone else? No one will think less of you if you didn't leave her even after you found out."

Milo groaned. "She denied anything was happening."

"So there *was* someone?"

"She seemed pretty interested in a guy she had class with," he admitted. "That's it."

Again, Dennis waited him out, and again Milo caved.

"She talked about him once in a while and even had me drive her to his house one time, which she claimed was to drop off school work, but sounded more like a manhunt to me."

"A manhunt?"

Milo sighed. "He had…gone missing."

Dennis raised his eyebrows and feigned surprise. "Missing?"

"Yeah, I'm not really interested in talking more about it."

"What was his name?"

"His *name*?" Milo shook his head. "Why does that matter?"

"Because I would like to know if she's moved on with him after you and her broke up."

"I don't think she did."

"But you don't know for sure."

Milo was quiet again.

"Come on," Dennis pushed. "Save me from getting involved with a girl who doesn't know the meaning of 'exclusive.' I'm not interested in anyone who is going to date around when she's with me.."

"She's not that kind of girl."

"Then there's no harm in you telling me that guy's name from her class. Just to verify that she's not talking to him anymore."

Milo studied him a moment before answering. "It was Harry."

"Harry who?"

He shrugged. "I don't know."

"We work with three different Harry's at the office," Dennis lied. "You have to give me more than that. You said she had you take her to his house? Where does he live? Maybe that'll narrow down the Harry's in our office."

"Where did you say you worked again?"

"It's some regional branch," Dennis lied again, hoping Milo hadn't been keeping tabs on Kathy to catch him in his fib. "It's a large office. The point is, there's a big fish of people to choose from."

"I don't know, I think it was Stough Avenue or something. Over near I-79. Look, you're not going to beat him up, are you?"

Dennis chuckled. "Of course not. Just curious. Thought I'd reach out to Harry personally."

Milo shook his head. "I don't think I'd do that if I were you. Harry...I don't think Harry has fond memories of Kathy. Honestly, some of mine aren't great—she's a nice girl, but..."

"But what?"

Milo shrugged, but his face lit up when the young girl came by with their food.

"Turkey club here, and chicken tenders for you." She slid her hands in her back pockets. "Ketchup and mustard are on the table. So is the hot sauce. Anything else I can get for you boys?"

Both men shook their heads and thanked her.

Dennis picked at his French fries, another attempt at trying not to come off as a threat at all. "Sounds like things ended pretty badly for you two."

"You could say that," Milo said. "Like I said, I don't really want to talk about it."

"I understand. It's just…I heard something else about Kathy. That she—well, her and her sister—have had some weird things happening around them."

Milo's head snapped up. "Weird?"

"Yeah. Her friend Trisha said that you went through some pretty traumatic stuff because of Kathy."

"Kathy's a nice person," Milo said. "What happened…it's just what happened. And you can't always rely on Trisha's word. She tends to exaggerate."

"I gathered that, but let's back up for a minute. What happened was…*devastating* for you, wasn't it?"

"I don't know what you're talking about, and I don't appreciate you grilling me."

The obvious lie brought a slight smirk to Dennis's lips, which Milo missed because he kept his head down on his food.

"Kathy has a good heart and she only wants what's best for everyone," Milo went on. "If anything, her only problem is that she cares *too* much."

"But that still wasn't enough for what happened to you."

Milo grabbed a napkin and wiped his hands. He scooted to

the end of the booth and stood. "You know what? I'm not interested in vilifying Kathy for you."

"Hey, that's not what I'm trying to do here," Dennis said. His heart raced as he worried that Milo was about to blow his whole pseudo-investigation. What if he went to Kathy and told her he was asking about her? What if he called Detective O'Leary?

"No, that's *exactly* what you're trying to do." Milo dug out some bills from his pocket and tossed them on the table. "Don't ever call me again."

Dennis watched him leave, panicked that the sisters—the *witches*—were going to get him before he could dig up any real dirt on them. If they found out he was looking into them, would they go after his parents to get back at him? Even if Samantha was about to deliver a devil spawn, he presumed she could still work her magic. She probably didn't even have to be *near* his parents to inflict pain on them.

But at least he had one thing he could use: he could hunt down Harry and find out what exactly he knew.

CHAPTER 30

- AUGUST 1989 -
- WASHINGTON, DC -

The girl whizzed by Dennis in a flash near Marion Park late at night. Seconds later, another man followed, concealed in the night sky by his dark clothing. Soon after, a second man raced by Dennis just as quick as the other two runners.

Dennis had been on his way back to the Navy Yard from a friend's apartment in DC, but no matter how tired he was, he could sense a bad vibe when it showed up. It didn't take long for him to make up his mind and follow the trio in his own sprint.

Zigzagging around rowhouse-lined city streets, Dennis managed to keep an eye on the runners even as they passed through shadows and around tight corners.

Eventually, they ended up down a dead-end alley behind several townhouses that had long turned out their lights for the night. Dennis lingered behind a brick garage and watched as the girl slowed to a stop at the end of the alley and realized that she was trapped.

Turning to the man in the black clothing, fear was very evident on her face.

"Please!" she begged. "Just leave me alone!"

But as the man in dark clothing stepped toward her, his body seemed to grow larger. Like a giant, he rose into the air, dwarfing the girl with his size.

She let out a shriek as she watched him take on a new shape.

The second man stepped behind the giant and called to the girl. "Get down!"

The man in the dark clothing turned at the sound of a second voice and snarled at the man.

The second man brought his hands together and jutted them out to the giant. The next thing Dennis knew, fire spewed from the man's hands directly at the giant.

Suddenly, the back of the rowhouses were illuminated brightly, casting new shadows around tiny garages and wooden fences.

As Dennis watched, his jaw clenched. Once again, he had discovered witches living among him. Were they everywhere? And look at what they were doing with that power! Terrifying women and disturbing a whole neighborhood of people.

In truth, Dennis wasn't sure if men could be considered witches, but the power that he witnessed was the same that he had witnessed before. *Witch* was the best way to describe them.

The giant shriveled to his regular size, then curled onto the brick alley and turned to ash. Only when he was gone, did the second man stop the stream of fire and put his hands down.

Both he and the girl locked eyes with each other.

"He's gone now," he called out to the girl. "Are you okay?"

Terror was still evident on the girl's face, but she nodded. With trembling breath, she murmured, "Thank you."

The man nodded back toward where Dennis was hiding. "Go on. Hurry home in case anyone else tries to chase you down tonight."

The girl didn't need any convincing. She raced by the man, only pausing when she noticed Dennis hiding behind one of the garages. She eyed him cautiously, then proceeded back out onto the street and out of sight.

Curious, Dennis watched the man as he maintained his stance, looking toward the end of the alley all by himself.

"I know you saw everything," he called to Dennis.

That surprised Dennis, but in the pursuit it had been hard to maintain his cover. Now that he had been called out, there was no reason to hide anymore. Dennis stepped out into the center of the alley, keeping a safe distance between him and the man. Although, if the man could throw fire, there was no such thing as a "safe distance."

"Can I trust you to keep this a secret?" the man turned his head so Dennis could see his profile, but not make out any distinct features in the darkness.

"Keep what a secret?" Dennis asked. "The fact that you're a *freak*?"

The man sighed. "I'm not a freak. I'm just someone who saved a girl's life."

Dennis chuckled. "Please, how do I know you didn't send that giant thing after her in the first place? Maybe you just wanted to corner her to have your way with her but decided to play hero when you noticed me following."

The man turned and faced Dennis, but the darkness still prevented any clarity. "You and I both know that wasn't my intent."

"Only because I showed up. What if I hadn't been here? Then what?"

"Then she still would've been saved and I would be able to go home right away." The man was clearly growing tired of the conversation and attempted to walk out of the alley.

As he approached, Dennis grabbed him by the arm and swung a punch with his free hand.

The man ducked, evading the attack, and wormed his arm free from Dennis's grasp.

The two of them eyed each other, sizing the other up.

"You really don't want to start a fight with me." The man put up his hands, similar to what he had done to the giant.

"Like hell I don't," Dennis said. "I'm tired of freaks like you doing whatever you please." He reached around and pulled a pistol from his waistband and pointed it right at the man's chest. Ever since what happened in New Orleans, he carried a weapon whenever he could.

The man raised his hands defensively. "Hey! Take it easy!"

"Put your hands down!" Dennis demanded. "I know what you can do with them."

"You also know that I only use my power when I need to help someone. You *saw* me do it!"

"Put your hands down!"

"The only other time I use my power is to defend myself," the man went on, hands still raised. "If I'm threatened—"

"Put them *down!*"

The man smirked. "I don't think you're going to shoot. You don't have the guts, otherwise you would've done it by now." He dropped his hands.

"Don't move!" Dennis warned.

"Or what? Is that thing even loaded?" He rolled his eyes and took a step forward. "I'm tired. Stop wasting my time. I'm out of here."

By the second step, Dennis had fired the first shot. The man's eyes went wide by time the second shot was fired. The third shot was for good measure, although it landed square in the chest just like the first two bullets had.

The witch fell to the ground, eyes wide open in surprise.

As Dennis ran off, he didn't feel remorse or fear as he had with the other two witches he had killed. Instead, he felt satisfaction that there was one less freak in the world to do whatever they wanted.

He liked to think that he was restoring the world order.

CHAPTER 31

Samantha gripped Steven's hand tightly as another contraction passed. They had been growing progressively worse. Luckily, the doctors had begun to administer painkillers, but they were still saving the big ones for when it came time for delivery.

As she gritted her teeth to the pain, the door swung open and Mary Harper burst into the room.

"Grandma's here!"

Samantha couldn't help but glare at her mother-in-law. This was, most certainly, not the time.

"Not now, Mom," Steven muttered before turning back to his wife. "Just breathe through it, honey."

"Come on, dear, let's come back," Marty said as he peeked

his head inside the door and saw what was happening. Behind him, Samantha saw her sister.

"Let's give her a minute," Kathy added.

Mary hesitated in the doorway, an unimpressed look on her face. "If you think this is hard, just wait until that baby starts crowning."

"Mom!" Steven snapped.

The pain subsided and Samantha flopped back against the bed, sweat glistening on her forehead.

Mary took that as her cue to walk right up and give her son a hug, then Samantha, who only patted Mary on the back gently. It was all that she could muster when all she wanted to do was curse the old woman.

Turning, Mary slapped her son's arm. "Why didn't you call us the *moment* you left for the hospital!"

"Ow! I called as soon as I could!" Steven hunched his shoulders and backed away from his mother's attacks. "My first priority was getting Sam here!"

Mary looked back at Samantha. "How are you feeling, dear? Is my son taking good care of you?"

Samantha gave a faint smile. "Yes, he is." She was starting to feel a little overwhelmed with the sudden audience she had in the room.

"I see your family has found you," a nurse said from the doorway. She was different than the one who had escorted in Mary, Marty, and Kathy. "Was your brother able to find you?"

Samantha's eyes flickered to her sister and then back to the nurse. "My brother?"

Her face began to falter. "Yeah. He was asking for you downstairs. Said he didn't want to miss the birth of his first niece or nephew."

Mary laughed. "Oh, what a coincidence! There must be another Samantha having a baby!"

Marty laughed along, but no one else in the room seemed convinced.

"Did he give his name?" Kathy asked.

The nurse looked uncertain, likely nervous that she had done something wrong. "Uh…Dennis?"

Kathy looked to Samantha, whose eyes went wide.

Again, Mary laughed. "No! That's not her brother! He probably just told you that so you would let him up here. No, he's just an old college friend of Samantha's. We had a nice chat in the lobby."

Samantha felt hot for an entirely different reason.

Mary patted the end of Samantha's bed. "You'll learn. When you have a baby, people come out of the woodwork to see you!"

The nurse looked to Samantha for confirmation.

Faking a smile, Samantha said, "Yeah, sorry. Must've slipped my mind. Pregnancy brain and all."

The nurse smiled, relieved. "No worries! I completely understand."

"Thanks for everything," Samantha said, then offered a

wave, politely signaling that the nurse should leave them alone.

When the door shut behind her, Samantha looked to her husband, who had the same fear-stricken face that she did.

"So! Were you guys waiting long?" he asked his parents.

"Five, maybe ten minutes," his father told him.

Steven's mother rolled her eyes. "It sure felt like forever."

Kathy made eye-contact with her sister and then pointed out into the hall. Samantha gave one quick nod before Kathy disappeared out the door.

The younger witch found the nurse at the nurse's station. When she saw Kathy approach, she regained her remorseful look and said, "I'm so sorry about the confusion. I didn't realize—"

"How long ago was Dennis up here?" Kathy asked.

"I'm not sure. I saw him in the main lobby downstairs maybe an hour or so ago."

So this mystery man had been here for a while. Kathy figured it was probably the guy she saw in the waiting room around the corner when she got off the elevator.

"Is that a problem?" the nurse asked quietly.

"Well…" Kathy didn't want to make the nurse feel any worse, but she wanted to protect her sister more. "Sam and I actually don't have a brother. Actually, with Steven's parents here, our whole family is already here."

"Oh. But the grandma said that man was a friend…right?"

Kathy shook her head. "Unfortunately, no. We don't know

anyone by that name."

"Oh," the nurse repeated. Her eyes were wide as the fear spread across her face.

"Could you do me a favor and call security and make sure that man—Dennis—doesn't get anywhere near my sister's room?"

The nurse began reaching for the phone before Kathy even finished. "Yes, of course. I'm so sorry. I thought—I didn't mean—I'll call right now."

"Thank you." Kathy looked around at everyone else in the area. No sign of Dennis, but depending on what they were up against, he could've morphed into someone else. Or simply vanished into thin air. There was no telling what evil would want to stop another witch from entering the world.

CHAPTER 32

Dennis pulled onto Stough Avenue from West 32nd Street and slowed down. He had no idea which one was Harry's house. Unfortunately, Milo had caught on to Dennis's plan before he divulged that much—not that he probably remembered anyway.

On the way over, Dennis had been trying to figure out how he was going to find Harry's house. He considered looking in the phonebook, but without Harry's last name, it would be impossible to find his address.

Instead, as Dennis pulled down Stough, he decided to take a chance and pull up in front of the first house with the interior lights on. For the most part, the neighborhood looked friendly enough, so the likelihood of stumbling up to some drug dealer's house was slim. Still, he wished he had stopped back at his parents' house and picked up the pistol he had brought with him from the ship.

The woman who answered the door was an attractive middle-aged woman. She wore a sweatshirt and jeans, and her hair hung to one side along her shoulder.

With an alluring smile, she said, "Why hello. What did I do right to get you on my doorstep?"

Dennis noticed no ring on her left hand, so he decided to indulge in her flirting. "I assure you, dear, the pleasure is all mine. I was hoping I could have a moment of your time to chat."

"Honey, I wish you'd stay for longer than a moment. Come on in." She stepped aside to allow him entry, and closed the door behind him. "Take off your shoes. Let's go sit in the living room. I can get you coffee or something."

They were standing in an awkward entry hallway with linoleum flooring. Two half-walls flanked an entrance to the carpeted living room on the right, and two steps at the end of the hallway led up to the kitchen. Dennis presumed that down the hallway to the left were the bedrooms and bathroom. A standard ranch house, likely only about twenty or thirty years old.

"No, I don't want any trouble," he said. "I actually just stopped to ask for directions."

"Oh." She crossed her arms and leaned against the wall. "Who is it you're looking for, honey?"

"My lab partner." The lie rolled off his tongue so easily. "You see, I'm a student at Porreco College."

"Wow," she said with no enthusiasm in her voice. "Congrats for you. Smart and cute. It's like you've already won the lottery."

Dennis grinned—that much was genuine. "Anyway, we exchanged contact information, but I didn't write anything down, which was a stupid move. Numbers don't really stick in my head very well so I completely forgot his phone number and address. I did remember Stough Avenue, though!"

The woman ran one hand through her hair, fluffing it up. She stuck out her hip seductively. "Well, you've found it. What's your partner's name? I don't know a lot of my neighbors, but maybe I can help you."

"Um…I know his first name is Harry. Not sure about his last name. He's about my age, maybe a smidge younger."

She threw her head back and laughed. "You lucked out, sweetie! I'm pretty sure that's my neighbor. Come here, and I'll show you." She stepped to the door and opened it. "Come in here real close and we can keep each other warm. Don't be shy now."

Dennis complied, smelling the shampoo in her hair as he did.

She pointed two houses down across the street to another squat ranch—all the houses on the street really did look the same. "The Reynolds' live just over there. They have a son named Harry, who I think is about your age. But as far as I know, he's not in college."

"Oh. So maybe that's not the one I'm looking for," Dennis muttered for her benefit, but still he wondered if that was the right Harry.

"Who knows? Maybe it is. I'm not sure." She looked up at him, her face inches from his in their close proximity. "He was a great student, the biggest brag those folks of his had. Then about a year or so ago, something changed. They just stopped talking about him. Claim he's taking a break from college to try to figure out what he wants to do with his life, but I'm not buying it. I mean, I don't have a college degree, but dropping out in the middle of the semester tells me that something happened, and not that he's just a confused young man. And to never see him outside anymore?" She shook her head. "It's just weird."

"Hmm," Dennis said. "Well, I'll go over and see if they can point me in the right direction. Even if he's not the right Harry on Stough Avenue I'm looking for, maybe they'll know where the other one is."

The woman laughed and swatted at Dennis's chest. "Oh, you're smart, cute, *and* funny. Are you single? Oh hell, does it matter?"

Dennis smiled politely. "I should probably go. Thank you for all of your help."

"Oh, do you have to go so soon?" She ran her hand down his arm and gripped his hand.

She was attractive enough and for a moment, Dennis

considered taking her up on her offer. All the other guys who were on leave took advantage of the young women up for a one-night-stand, but Dennis had to find Harry.

"Thanks again for your help." He moved passed her and stepped out into the cold. He offered her a wave before turning and walking across the street to the house she had pointed out. He had to protect his parents. If there was something bad about those girls—those *witches*—he needed to figure it out before his parents became one of their next casualties.

CHAPTER 33

When Kathy turned to return to her sister's hospital room, she stopped when she saw Steven exiting the room and closing the door behind him. With a tilt of his head, he indicated that she should follow him to the empty waiting room down the hall.

Once alone, he leaned in close to her and muttered in a hushed tone, "Is this something we need to worry about?"

"I don't know. I told the nurse at the desk to notify security to make sure he doesn't come up here again. I'm hoping it's harmless, but you never know."

"So my mother *was* talking to him?"

Kathy nodded. "I saw them when I came back up just now. I tried not to let the guy see me, but I didn't really have anywhere to hide."

Steven stood back and ran his hands through his hair as he let out a deep breath. He was clearly exhausted. Kathy could see bags under his bloodshot eyes. His hair, which was usually so perfectly combed over, was a mess.

"So he was up here?" he asked.

"Yeah, but after your parents went to go to Sam's room, the guy just walked back to the elevators and left. It was weird." She paused, then asked, "The nurse said his name was Dennis? That name sounds so familiar."

"Samantha and I had dinner with the neighbors across the street last night," Steven said. "Their son Dennis came home in the middle of it. Samantha must've told you about it."

She nodded. "That's right. I remember now. What did he look like?"

"A little younger than us, built, shaved head—he's in the Navy."

Kathy glanced over at the nurse's station. Many of them were stealing glances their way. The potential intruder was obviously the latest gossip. "Sounds like the guy I saw."

"Why do you think he was looking for Samantha? He didn't seem to like her at all last night. Actually, Samantha didn't seem to like him, either. But he came over this morning and apologized for everything that was said. I thought that was the end of it."

"I don't kn—" Kathy stopped herself. "Wait, which house

did you say his parents lived in?"

"The one right across the street. The Kors' house."

Kathy's eyes grew wide. "The same one where the Halloween party was!"

"The party from hell where I was kept prisoner for two days?"

"Yes, the one where we killed the shapeshifter." She sighed. "I wonder if he's putting the clues together."

"So is he magical?"

She shrugged. "I don't know. Maybe. Doesn't sound like it, though."

"I can tell Samantha's stressed out about it," he said. "And the fact that I just left her with my parents doesn't help. She feels useless and scared, which is why she's been so cranky lately."

"To be fair, she's about to have a baby, so being cranky is within her right," Kathy said. "Although she has been kind of out of line today especially."

"I caught her earlier trying to use her powers to get more meds."

She rubbed her forehead. "That can't happen."

"I know. I yelled at her for it. But there's so much on her plate right now and this potential intruder isn't helping." He looked back down the hall at the closed door to Samantha's room. "I should get back to her before my mother says anything rude."

"And I'll see if I can check into who Dennis is and what he

wants," Kathy said. "There's a chance that he knows too much about us and about what happened in that house. Tell Samantha that I'm taking care of it and that I'll be back as soon as I can."

To her surprise, Steven pulled her in for a hug. "Thanks, Kathy. I know you want to be here for your sister, but you're the only one who can take care of this for us."

She patted him on the back and then pulled away. "I know, but it's part of my job. Keep everyone safe, especially my family."

Steven rolled his neck back, which popped in response. "This was definitely not the way I wanted to bring my first child into the world."

Kathy chuckled. "Do you even know who you married?"

CHAPTER 34

"Can I help you?" It was an older woman who answered the door. Middle-aged, sporting a pink housecoat and matching slippers that had seen better days. Her graying hair was wet, slicked back from what was apparently a recent shower.

"Hi," Dennis said with a smile. "I was wondering if I could speak to Harry?"

The woman's face darkened. "Oh. Are you a reporter?"

What was with everyone thinking he was a reporter?

He looked down and smirked again. "No, I'm not. My parents live in the house where Harry…" He paused, wondering how direct he could be. Might as well go for it and see what her reaction was. He didn't have time to waste on pleasantries wrapped around a fictional story. "Where he was held captive. I was hoping to talk to Harry to get his perspective on the whole experience."

The woman began to close the front door, leaving Dennis on the front stoop. "We're not interested—"

From deeper inside the house, a voice called out, "Let him in."

The woman studied Dennis again, but opened the door and allowed him to enter.

Dennis followed the woman into the carpeted living room. It was dark, with only a floor lamp lit behind the recliner where a man sat. The curtains were pulled tight, which Dennis assumed were like that all day long. At the opposite end of the room sat a large television set, playing a sci-fi movie.

The person sitting in the recliner was not who Dennis had pictured for Harry. He was overweight, wearing a soiled T-shirt that had once been white and worn red flannel pajama bottoms. From the smell of body odor, Dennis judged that it had been at least a couple days since Harry had gotten up to take a shower. And, judging from the piles of empty wrappers and pop cans around the chair, Dennis could tell what Harry's diet had consisted of.

Dennis stepped forward and extended his hand. "Harry? I'm Dennis Kors. I hope to not take up too much of your time tonight."

Harry turned down the sound on the TV with the remote

and shook Dennis's hand. "It's okay. It'll actually be a change to my routine for once."

His mother fussed over him, cleaning up wrappers, picking up empty cans, and folding the blanket that had fallen to the floor.

"Mom, could you go make us something to eat?" Harry suggested. "Give us some time to talk?"

The woman studied Dennis, then turned to her son. "What would you like, sweetie?"

Harry turned to their visitor. "Do you have a preference?"

Dennis put up his hands in protest. "No, don't worry about me. I just ate." He noticed the look Harry was giving him, telling him to let the woman run this errand. "But I'm sure whatever you whip up will be just fine."

"Why don't you fix us up some of that cobbler you made last night?" Harry suggested. "If there's any left."

"I think there is some leftover from what you had at lunch," she said. "I'll check."

"Thanks, Mom."

She disappeared through a doorway beside the TV.

When they were alone, Harry said, "Sorry about that. She's been overprotective since…*it* happened. Actually, it even drove a wedge between my parents. My dad actually just moved out right before Thanksgiving. I'm sure the divorce papers are coming soon."

"I'm sorry to hear that."

"If it wasn't broke to begin with, it never would've fell apart that quickly." He motioned to the couch. "Have a seat."

Dennis sat and folded his hands together. "I understand that this is a sensitive topic, so I appreciate you taking the time to discuss it with me."

"What brings you by?" Harry asked. "Most people would rather I didn't talk about it. Either they think it was some sadistic kidnapping where I was drugged, or they think I'm making the whole thing up."

"For what it's worth, I believe you."

Offering a half-hearted smile, Harry said, "Thanks. It helps. So what made you want to come talk to me?"

"My parents live in the house where you were held captive," Dennis started. "My chief concern are a couple of the neighbors. Two women who live across the street from the house."

Harry nodded. "I think I know who you're talking about."

"Would you mind talking about it with me?" Dennis asked. "I don't want to cross any lines. I hope you're okay with helping me out."

"Sure." Harry shrugged. "I've been working through it. Slowly. Mom finally sent me to a therapist so I could talk about what happened without just getting sympathy from people in my life. Over the last year it seems like it's almost taboo to talk about it, even when I'm okay with it. I guess my mom is dealing with it in her own way too, so having someone other than my shrink to talk about it is refreshing."

"I have to be honest with you that I'm fuzzy on the details," Dennis said. "Could you tell me exactly what happened?"

Harry sighed and stared at the TV as he recalled. He turned down the sound, then started. "It was right before Halloween. I had just gotten out of class at Porreco College and I was walking back to my car." He paused for a moment, likely fighting through his memories. "I felt someone grab me from behind. I turned around and saw what I thought was this guy."

"What do you mean you *thought* he was a guy?"

"He was a guy when he grabbed me. Punched me out and threw me in the backseat of my own car and drove off with me." He shook his head. "Woke up in some basement, tied up to the rafter. The weirdest part was that I caught him."

"*Caught* him?"

"Caught him changing," Harry clarified. "At that point he had had his clothes off, but then he started pulling at his skin too." He made a face of revulsion. "It was disgusting. He was ripping it right off of him!"

"He was pulling his *skin* off?"

Harry nodded. "Freaky, right? Anyway, that wasn't even the weirdest part. His whole body started convulsing and then he…" He shook his head. "I don't know, exactly, but within a few minutes he looked just like me."

Dennis narrowed his eyes in disbelief. "He was a clone?"

"Something like that. I'm not really sure what that…*thing* was, but all I know is it could change shape. Over the next couple days, it came back and did the same thing over and over again. Strip off its clothes, pull off its skin, then morph into someone else. It would pull on different clothes and go on as if that was completely normal."

"What about the girls? The neighbors, Samantha and Kathy. How did they fit into this, exactly?"

Harry shook his head. "I don't know, but that thing changed into them too. Well, Samantha at least. Anyway, they knew what to do with that thing. How to take care of him, which I was grateful for. At one point, Samantha was overpowered by the thing and dragged down to the basement with us but Kathy came down and rescued us."

"Rescued how?" Dennis asked, but his question got lost with Harry's mother's return.

"Here's the cobbler, dear." She handed her son a large portion and Dennis a considerably smaller one.

"This looks so good!" Harry cheered as he greedily dug into his helping.

Dennis politely picked at his, especially as Harry's mother stood by and watched them eat.

"You know what would go good with this?" Harry asked. "Ice cream. Do we have any, Ma?"

She nodded. "There should be some in the freezer in the garage. Let me go check." Once again, she ducked out into the kitchen and left the two of them alone.

Dennis set aside his cobbler. "So what exactly happened to

that thing that took you? I'd hate to think it's still roaming around hunting people down and…*morphing* into them."

Harry scooped up the last of his dessert and shook his head. "No need to worry about that. The thing's gone. The sisters…did something. Cast a spell or something. I'm not sure. All I know is that he *melted*. Like, totally melted like cheese. I've never seen anything like it."

"So they're witches?" Dennis asked, just to confirm what he had already deduced.

Again, Harry shrugged. "I guess. Hey, if they're going to hunt down more things like that, then let them be witches. I don't mind. They saved my life."

"But it's because of them that you were subjected to that kind of torment," Dennis said. "Aren't you upset with them?"

"I mean, I guess I can see your point, but no. I'm not mad at them. I'm grateful. Like I said, they saved my life." Harry pointed his fork at Dennis. "What scares me is how long it went on before they knew about it. I mean, what else is crawling around the world that they haven't stopped yet? They're only two women, how are they supposed to stop all of the evil in the world? I'd rather stay right here where it's safe."

With a judgmental look, Dennis figured that Harry's decision to sit would soon become a necessity if he kept up all of his eating. But he kept that theory to himself.

Harry's mother came back with a nearly-empty plastic tub of ice-cream. "We only have fudge swirl left. I'll have to add mint chocolate chip to the shopping list because we're out."

"Thanks Mom. Fudge swirl will do."

She smiled and then disappeared into the kitchen to dish it out.

Dennis rose to his feet. "All right, well, I think I've taken up enough of your time. Thank you for talking to me. I appreciate it."

Harry offered his hand. "You're welcome. My therapist says talking about this will help me overcome it."

"Keep at it." After they shook hands again, Dennis couldn't resist adding one piece of advice. "And maybe consider going outside when the weather is nice again. The sunshine and the movement might help you feel better."

CHAPTER 35

As soon as Kathy stepped into the house—her *sister's* house, she had to remind herself—she felt that something was off. With each lamp she switched on, she didn't immediately notice anything, but her witch intuition was screaming out all kinds of alerts.

Kathy tried to assure herself that what was different was that Samantha had slowly began to claim the house as her own, making subtle changes like swapping out old portraits, refreshing vases, and burning different scented candles. Despite the efforts to calm herself, a nagging feeling persisted in her mind.

Upstairs, Kathy entered the room that had once been her bedroom. It was still mostly empty, although Samantha had cleaned up the dust trails and straightened the leftover boxes.

Being back in her former bedroom brought a sad pang of nostalgia to Kathy. At that moment, she wished she still lived in the house and everything had been the same as it always had been. But she knew that wasn't right. That was the easy solution. Change was good, but change was also hard.

Shaking off her emotion, Kathy crossed the room to search under the boxes for the magic book. When she had moved out, she had left it in her room. Judging by the fact that Kathy could no longer find it, she figured her sister had moved it to a better hiding place. Kathy checked the closet, but it was empty, except for a few old wire hangers.

Kathy went to Samantha's room next and searched under her bed, in her closet, by her nightstand. Every spot came up empty for the magic book.

She wouldn't have put it in the baby's room, she thought to herself.

On a whim, Kathy went back downstairs and searched the bookshelves in the living room. Admittedly, it was a long shot. Samantha was paranoid about people finding out that they were witches. She wouldn't present their magical tome in a room that saw a lot of traffic by non-magical people. But there was a collection of other old books in the living room, so Kathy thought there was a chance it could be hiding in plain sight.

When she checked, though, she couldn't find anything. Worse, that feeling that something was off nagged at her again.

Then she felt it: the house was colder than it usually was. Despite all of their bickering, that was the one thing the sisters could agree on about living together. They both liked a toasty house.

Kathy investigated further, checking the doors into the sunroom—locked and insulated for the winter. When she stepped into the dining room, the chill was more pronounced, like a draft. She followed it into the kitchen, where the first thing she noticed was that the back door was slightly open.

It was an old house and Kathy knew that if the back door hadn't been closed just right, it was very possible for it to swing back open.

Crossing the room, she shut the door and locked it. The next feeling that hit her was fear. She was *sure* they had locked the door before they left for the hospital. So how was it open?

Was someone in the house with her?

Moving back through the house slowly, Kathy checked every potential hiding place for an intruder. She listened carefully, trying to hear any footsteps on the squeaky floorboards upstairs, but the whole house was silent. That fact didn't help Kathy relax, but actually made her more apprehensive. It meant that someone could be lying in wait for her, possibly even watching her at that very moment.

When she made it back to the living room, something out the front window caught her eye. Dennis had just pulled up to the curb in front of the house across the street. He shot out of his car and ran up the steps to the front door, passing through the shadows between the streetlight and the Kors' porch light.

Kathy let out a heavy sigh.

Of course, she thought. *The open door. Lurking at the hospital. Asking around about us. Dennis was probably the one who broke in.*

She watched as he disappeared into the house across the street.

"I'll figure out what you're up to," she muttered to herself.

CHAPTER 36

When Dennis burst through the front door of his parents' house, they both jolted awake in the living room.

"Dennis?" his mother called to him as he tried to beeline it up the stairs. "Come back here. Where have you been?"

Slumping his shoulders, he returned to the living room. The Christmas tree was still on, as was the light above the nativity scene beneath it. The TV played whatever game show they happened to be watching. Dennis didn't pay much attention. He wanted to get in and get out as quickly as possible. Suddenly, the knowledge of what had truly happened on that street—in that *house*—was too much for him and he didn't want to spend another second in it. His parents would be okay in their ignorance, as long as he took care of the two people who knew were responsible for bringing that *thing* to the street anyway. If you allow one witch—one *freak*—to linger, that would only attract others.

"You've been gone most of the evening," his father added. "Skipped out on dinner."

"I have a plate for you in the fridge." Nancy began to rise from her seat. "I'll go warm it up for you."

"No, that's okay," Dennis said quickly. "I'm going to run out again soon."

"Where?" Gerald asked.

Dennis shrugged. "Just visiting friends." He averted his eyes, hating the idea of lying to them. But it was for their own protection!

Nancy stepped forward and cupped her son's face in her hands. She brought his head down and kissed his forehead. "That's very nice of you, dear. I'm sure you had plenty to catch up on. We just wish you'd told us, that's all."

"Or called," his father grumbled. He clicked the TV off with the remote, threw back the throw blanket he had on over himself, and hauled himself out of the recliner with a grunt. "We're just glad you're okay. You going back to your friends' then?"

Dennis nodded once, which he rationalized as something that could be passed off as an agreement or simply an acknowledgment. It was his way of justifying the lies.

"Which friend?" Nancy asked.

"Evan and the guys." It was the first group he could recall off the top of his head. He hadn't seen most of them, or really talked to any of them, in a couple years.

"That'll be nice to catch up with some of the old neighborhood," Nancy said. "Have their mothers call me. I would like to visit with them myself."

"Yes, ma'am." More evasion. More lies.

Nancy squeezed his arm as she passed by him. "Don't stay out too late. Love you, sweetie. Good night!"

"'Night," he mumbled.

Gerald studied his son as he waited for Nancy to get up the stairs. When she reached the second floor, he leaned in closer to Dennis and whispered, "You're not doing anything illegal, are you?"

"No, sir." Dennis swallowed the guilt down. Killing two women certainly *was* illegal, but what other choice did he have? He couldn't let two witches live across from his parents and attract more mysterious murderers to his parents' new neighborhood.

"Good." Gerald patted his son on the shoulder as he walked by. "Just be safe. Good night, son. Love you."

"Love you too."

Dennis waited for his parents' bedroom door to close before he ventured up to his guest room. Sitting on his bed was the large book he had taken from across the street. Beside it sat his bag.

He dug through his clothes in his duffel until he found his pistol. After what he heard from his friends who had started being deployed to Panama, he wanted to have a weapon available to him at all times, just in case.

Stashing the gun in the waistband of his jeans and fixing his shirt and jacket to conceal it, Dennis took one last look around the room to determine if he needed anything else. On a whim, he decided to throw the covers over the book. The last thing he needed were his parents stumbling upon it and assuming *he* was the practitioner.

Satisfied, he made his way back down the stairs and out to his car. He needed to get back to that hospital to take care of the witches.

CHAPTER 37

It took a while for Gerald Kors to answer the door when Kathy rang the bell, but when he did he was still tying the bathrobe around his large belly.

"Can I help you?" he asked.

She smiled politely. "Hi, I'm Kathy Walker. I used to live across the street. My sister still lives there with her husband. I'm sorry for coming over so late." She looked passed Gerald and saw Nancy standing on the stairs in her own robe.

"Kathy?" the old woman asked, coming to the door. "Come in, out of the cold!"

Gerald sighed heavily, but let their guest pass by him, shutting the door behind her.

When the door shut, Kathy opened her hands and froze the

two of them. She couldn't risk freezing them with the door open. It had started to snow and the last thing she wanted to do was call attention to her magic by bringing a chill to the room or a pile of snow wafting through the front door.

With her magic in effect, Kathy darted up the stairs. Before coming over, she had watched Dennis leave and race off just as fast as he had arrived. He was in a hurry and Kathy didn't like it.

Upstairs, she was first hit with the memories of that Halloween party the year before. She and Samantha had snuck up to check out the bedrooms. Down the hall in the master was where they had found the first physical sign of the shapeshifter: the vat of skin he left behind.

Her body shook with chills at the memory.

Hoping she wouldn't have to reenter that room, she started with the first bedroom at the top of the stairs.

Inside, there wasn't much to see, although she was sure that it was the room Dennis had been staying in. The bed was ruffled, even though there was no other sign of him. Didn't they teach you to make your bed in the Navy?

Kathy tried a couple of drawers, looked in the closet, and inspected under the bed. None of it revealed anything.

Sighing, she started to head back into the hall. She wasn't sure what she expected to find anyway. Some sort of clue—evidence—of what he was up to, maybe? Obviously, that was stupid. If Dennis was truly a threat, then he wouldn't leave a trail for her to find.

Before she left, a thought occurred to her. Turning, she returned to the bed and pulled off the blanket. She let out a gasp when she saw what lay underneath.

The magic book.

She stared in disbelief for a few seconds, but there it was. Right in front of her. The realization of what that meant came flooding over her.

Dennis had definitely been in their house.

Dennis knew they were witches.

And Dennis intended to hurt them.

It had been just about a year since Kathy had witnessed the full exposure of their magic, which had led to catastrophic outcomes. And she did not want to repeat that.

Another thought occurred to her: Dennis needed to be stopped.

Tucking the book under her arm, she carried it downstairs. Her magic would likely be wearing off at any time, so she needed to move quick.

She retook her position, trying not to bring attention to the fact that she now carried a book. She hoped that they wouldn't notice when they unfroze.

"What brings you over this late?" Nancy asked after Kathy's magic faded. "How's your sister?"

"She's doing okay. Things are going slow, but they're going. Everything and everyone seem healthy. I actually stopped at the house to get a, um, change of clothes and I just thought I'd pop over and give you guys an update."

"Oh, how nice," Nancy said with a warm smile.

"What have you got there?" Gerald asked, indicating the book.

"Oh, just some reading for Samantha," Kathy played it off. "I should be getting back to her. Don't want that baby born without me. Sorry to wake you." She reached for the doorknob.

"Would you like to stay for tea?" Nancy asked.

Kathy shook her head. "I really do need to get going, but I appreciate the offer. How about a rain check? We can have tea and play cards next weekend after the baby comes."

"I'll look forward to it."

"Good night!" Kathy called to them as she stepped into the cold.

"Give your sister our best!" Nancy called with a wave before closing the door.

Kathy was grateful to get out of the house, only so she could stop their lunatic son. She didn't believe that they knew what he was up to. If they did, would he turn his anger on them? She needed to protect her sweet old neighbors, even if they weren't *technically* her neighbors anymore.

Her feet crunched in the snow as she made her way back to Samantha's car. Even as she started it up, pulled on her seatbelt, and pulled away from the curb, her mind raced with thoughts of Dennis.

He would probably go back to the hospital. He would

probably try to get close to Samantha. Would he be successful now that security had been alerted to him?

What worried her the most was this: Dennis wasn't necessarily in a hurry because he knew that as long as Samantha was in labor, she wasn't going anywhere. She was a sitting duck.

CHAPTER 38

Samantha looked much more tired when Kathy returned to the hospital. Her hair was pulled up into a loose bun on the top of her head, the errant strands that didn't stay in place clung to her forehead with sweat, which accentuated the dark spots under her eyes.

"There you are," Samantha said with a sleepy smile when she saw Kathy come through the door. She didn't even pick her head up from the pillow. "I was wondering where you went."

"Just needed to take care of some stuff." Kathy's eyes flickered over to Steven, who noticed that she wanted to get his attention.

"Nothing magical, I hope." Samantha rolled her head to the other side and closed her eyes.

"Are you going to make it?" Kathy avoided her sister's question by presenting one of her own. "You haven't had the baby yet, have you?"

Steven shook his head. "No baby, but they said it could be soon so the doctors gave her some stronger meds."

"I feel great." Samantha didn't even open her eyes, but her smile was ever-present.

"Well, get some rest," Kathy advised. "You're going to need it real soon." She looked over at Steven. "Can we talk for a sec?"

He followed her out into the hall and closed the door behind him.

"Where'd your parents go?" Kathy turned and looked down the hall to the maternity waiting room. "I don't see them."

"They went down to grab a coffee from the cafeteria," he said. "Mom decided to break her no-caffeine-after-three rule just so she could be awake for when the baby comes."

Kathy rolled her eyes. "Great. So she'll be even more irritable."

"She *is* my mother," Steven said. "And this *is* her first grandchild. I think she has a right to want to be here for it."

Sarcasm was on the tip of Kathy's tongue, but she had the presence of mind to stop herself from offering a scathing retort. Steven had bags under his eyes. Kathy could feel herself swaying with the weight of her body. They were all exhausted and their fuses were much shorter than usual.

Instead, she took a deep breath and said, "You're right. I'm sorry. I'm just frustrated that I have to put up with this. Can't we have one special occasion that isn't screwed up by someone who wants to kill us?"

"Is that what you found out? Is that what Dennis wants? Is that why he was here?"

She nodded. "I think so. Someone was in the house since we've been here and when I went over to investigate at the Kors'—"

"You told them what happened?"

"No, I froze them and snuck into the house without them knowing. Anyway, I found our magic book in their guest room."

Steven's eyes grew wide as her words finally sunk in. "He was in our house? How did he get in?"

"Back door in the kitchen. He must've picked the lock."

"That's it. I'm replacing those old locks."

"They're antiques. You can't just rip them out of the house."

"Well, they're obviously unsafe."

"Just because one jackass got into the house doesn't mean you need to throw out the history in the house. Maybe the lock just needs to be greased up or something."

Steven crossed his arms and leaned against the wall. "Something needs to happen. I'm not bringing home my newborn baby and recovering wife if the doors don't even lock."

Kathy could've pointed out that half of what they were usually up against didn't always need to use the doors, but she let it pass. He didn't need anymore stress on his plate. Besides, talking about door locks was so far off topic.

"Anyway," she said. "Judging by what he found and the way he's been asking around, I have a theory that he wants to hurt us. Maybe even the baby."

Steven stood straighter and dropped his arms to his sides. "He wouldn't."

"He's going to try, but he's not going to succeed," Kathy said. "I'm going to stop him."

"By yourself?"

"Do I have any other option?"

He sighed. "No, I guess not. Do you even know what kind of powers he has?"

She shook her head. "I'm not sure he has any. His parents obviously don't. Samantha and I would've picked up on that fact over the last year if they did."

"So he's a witch hunter then?"

She shrugged. "I guess so. It's not every day the nonmagical go after the magical, so there's not really a term for it. But yes, if we're borrowing from Salem in the 1600s, then sure. He's a witch hunter."

"So how are you going to stop him?"

Kathy let out a deep breath and looked down at the floor. "I don't know." After a noticeable pause, she looked back up into his eyes and said, "All I know is that he definitely needs to be stopped. Somehow."

CHAPTER 39

Once Kathy had recognized her exhaustion, that was all that she could feel. It was like a fog had been cast on her mind, blocking out her normal perceptions and intuitions.

She passed through the main lobby of the hospital, nearly dismissing the conversation between a man and a security guard that she heard in passing. Only when she heard the word "sister" did her attention turn.

"…need to see my sister," one man pleaded. The voice sounded familiar to Kathy. A moment later, it hit her: Dennis.

The security guard shook his head. "No sir. I've been given strict orders that you are not allowed up on maternity."

Kathy tried not to act conspicuous, although she hooked around the front desk and took a seat in the waiting room of the main lobby. Grabbing a newspaper from the table beside her, she lifted it up and tried her best to conceal her face so she could listen in on the rest of the conversation.

"You're not going to let me be up there for my sister when she has her baby?" Dennis asked.

The guard chuckled. "That's the thing. She's not your sister. And if you're going to argue about the lie you were caught in, perhaps I need to escort you down the hall to the psychiatric services."

Kathy smirked at that.

"Who told you she wasn't my sister?" Dennis asked.

"She did. She told the nurse upstairs that she doesn't even have a brother."

"So maybe she's the one who needs to see the shrink and not me."

Kathy had to hand it to him. He stuck to his story.

"Look," the guard said, "the bottom line is, you're not going up there. End of story. Now, I can escort you to your car or we can involve the police. You make your choice."

Dennis grumbled, but started off toward the door. The security guard watched him go, but another hospital worker walked up to him and asked him a question. As Kathy lowered the newspaper, she noticed that Dennis had picked up on the security guard's distraction and was using it to his advantage. Instead of exiting the hospital, he turned down a hall, around the corner from the security guard and out of sight.

Kathy looked from where Dennis had disappeared to and where the security guard stood, hoping that he would pick up on the fact that Dennis didn't actually leave. But the guard was engrossed in the conversation with the hospital worker, so Kathy threw the newspaper aside and shot to her feet to follow Dennis herself.

As she rounded the corner, she caught glimpses of him snaking around the labyrinth maze that the hospital had become with several additions and renovations over the years.

Finally, she caught up with him at the end of a long hallway of offices. Most of the rooms were dark, with it being well after working hours. At the end of the hallway, Kathy whipped open the door she had seen Dennis escape through seconds before and nearly fell as she stumbled onto a landing at the top of a concrete staircase.

Below her, she could hear footsteps moving fast. Dennis wasn't far away.

She broke into a run, rushing down the stairs herself. At the bottom, she entered the maintenance corridor, which had been deserted by the first shift crew. Somewhere around the corner, a radio station played classic rock, but no one was in sight.

Kathy's pace slowed as she moved down the corridor. She hadn't heard Dennis enter any of the rooms she passed by, all of which had closed doors and dark windows.

Rounding another corner, she came upon a hallway. It had been more finished that around the corner. There was tile on the floors and the drywall was painted the same beige color as everything upstairs. It was a stark contrast to the obvious cost-saving construction from where she had entered.

Down the hall, she heard a door crash open. Kathy broke into a run and followed the sound, pushing through a door into a darkened room. The first thing that hit her was the cold.

She looked around for any sight of Dennis, briefly wondering if she followed him into the next room. Then her thought was dispelled as she felt the distinct feeling of a gun pressed against the back of her head.

"Don't move."

CHAPTER 40

ennis?" Kathy asked with her hands raised. She didn't dare turn her head to confirm her thoughts.

"How long have you been on to me?"

"Just the last hour or two." She swallowed, trying to soothe her suddenly dry throat. "Ever since the nurse asked about our brother."

He groaned. "Ah, I knew one of my lies would come to bite me in the ass. Oh well, what can you do? The good thing is I was still able to get the upper-hand over you. You know, for someone who is apparently so powerful, you really have terrible hiding places. You think I didn't see you sitting there behind that newspaper?"

"What do you want?" She took in her surroundings, her

mind working overtime trying to keep Dennis talking while also formulating a plan. As her vision adjusted tot he darkness, she could make out a wall full of metal drawers in front of her. They were in the hospital morgue. "What did my sister and I ever do to you?"

"Nothing," he said plainly. "My issue is what you could do. After all, you live right across the street from my parents, and the previous owners of that house had a rather…unfortunate outcome."

"We didn't do anything to the people who lived there before your parents." It occurred to her that Dennis had lured her to the morgue because it was below ground and was well insulated. Nobody would hear the full blast of the gunshot and even if they did, by the time they got down to investigate, he would be long gone.

"No? Well then, let's talk about what exactly *did* happen that night." He moved around to her front, keeping the gun pointed right at her. "And don't leave out any details."

"Um…" Kathy murmured, desperately trying to recall the specifics of that particular event. "Well, the people who lived in the house before your parents were clients of Samantha's. She's an accountant. They had invited her and Steven to a party and, by extension, me too. It was a Halloween party."

"Yes, so I've heard."

"When we went, we realized that we never saw the couple together in the same room. Our dates also kept disappearing on us, which wasn't like them."

"You were dating Milo then, right?"

Kathy felt a chill come over her. What Milo had seen that night had certainly scarred him. She couldn't stand the thought of him being in anymore pain at her expense. "You didn't hurt him, did you? I swear, if you did—"

"Relax." Dennis continued to circle around her, keeping the gun pointed at her at all times. "All we had was a nice chat. And dinner. He's fine. Now go on."

"We went to investigate what was happening and we found…" She took a deep breath. How much was she really going to reveal? Anything to save her life—and her sister's. "We found some skin, which we later found out was from a shapeshifter."

"Shapeshifter? Refresh my mind on what kind of freak that is." He passed by her line of vision again.

"Someone who can turn into other people," she explained. "In this case, he turned into the people we noticed were missing from the party."

"The hosts and your dates."

She nodded.

"So tell me about what happened in the basement. That's where the murders were, correct?"

"Sounds like you already know the whole story."

From behind, he pushed the gun against her head again. "Forgive me for fact-checking."

Kathy winced, fighting the urge to cry out in fear. She considered using her power, but what good would that do? After the immediate threat was taken care of, the fact of the matter was that she didn't have anything on him. He would still be stalking them. Still be threatening them. Better to deal with this now, before the baby came and she risked putting him or her in danger too.

"My sister and I had separated," she explained. "I went to look in our magic book about what we were up against and she stayed at the party. When I came back, I couldn't find her. At least, not the *real* her. That's when I heard the noises coming from the basement and went down to check it out."

"How did you hear noises from the basement if there was a raging party?"

Kathy knew that he knew how she had heard. He wanted her to say it. Was he recording her? Or was this justifying his actions? A private trial where she had already been deemed guilty?

"I used my power," she said softly.

"I'm sorry? Couldn't hear that."

"I can freeze people in time," she said louder. "I froze the party and heard the hostages in the basement."

As he passed by her field of view again, he had a smirk on his face. "Go on."

"There were four hostages: my sister, her husband, Milo, and a kid I had class with. I tried to free them, but I didn't have time before the shifter came downstairs."

"And how did you stop him?"

"My sister and I said a spell."

"That did what, exactly?"

She gulped. "Killed him."

He came to a stop behind her and pressed the gun to her head again. "So with just a few flowery words, you were able to end someone's life. And why shouldn't I stop you if you wield that kind of power? Why shouldn't I stop your sister—or her baby, before they can grow up and become just exactly what you are?"

"Don't you touch that baby—or my sister," she warned.

"Or what? You'll put a spell on me too?"

"Maybe."

"I don't think so," he said. "See, I have this working theory, just judging from the people I've talked to today. Everything weird that's happened—mostly revolving around that night— has been when you and your sister are together. See, I believe you only have power when you're with your sister. Perhaps that's why you haven't put a spell on me yet."

Good, she thought to herself. *Let him believe I'm powerless without Samantha. Let him put his guard down so I can use my magic on him.*

"Still," he went on, "even if you can't perform magic without your sister, you've been pretty manipulative in your life. People around you seem worse off having known you."

"What happened that night was terrible, but it wasn't my fault," she said. "As soon as Sam and I knew what was going on, we helped those people."

"And now look at them. Milo wants nothing to do with you. Harry is verging on morbidly obese, still living with his mother. And Steven is now forever tied to you and your sister simply because he's the father of her child. That's not to mention the previous owners of my parents' house having died or Harry's parents being driven to divorce after what happened to him."

"Neither of those things were our fault."

"Weren't they?" he shouted, pressing the gun against her skull so hard that it hurt. "If it weren't for you and the other freaks that exist in this world, none of that would've happened!"

With a shaky voice, she tried to defend herself, "If it weren't for us, all of them would've died—maybe everyone at that party. We help people. That's our job as witches."

"If that's true, then why did people still die? Either you're not good at what you claim to do or you simply don't care."

"That's not—we can't be expected to know everything! We do our best!"

"Well your best wasn't good enough!" he snarled.

"Please—" she started, but stopped when she heard a woman's voice call out behind them.

"Freeze!"

As soon as Kathy felt the gun pull away from her head, she ducked to the ground and rolled away. Her body slammed into the wall of drawers, but she didn't have time to register exactly what lay on the other side.

A woman in a pantsuit had her gun raised at Dennis. Her coat was held back by the walkie talkie clipped to her belt, showcasing the gold badge at her waist.

Kathy recognized her as the detective who questioned her after that Halloween party.

Dennis raised his gun at the detective. She didn't take any chances and fired three shots at him, sending echoes ricocheting through the nearly empty room.

Kathy clutched at her ears to drown out the noise, but they still rang. What she saw, however, was Dennis's body convulsing from the bullets, then falling back to the tiled floor.

Dead.

CHAPTER 41

Kathy stared at the table in front of her blankly. She wasn't sure exactly where in the hospital she was. A break room of some sort. All she knew was that it was empty. And quiet, which was where the exhaustion had finally hit her full-force.

From the moment the gun was pressed against her head until that moment, everything had been a blur for her. She couldn't recall how much time had passed or who exactly she had talked to. Her whole conversation with Dennis had been stored into the confines of her mind, locked aware to help her cope with how close she had come to the brink of death.

Obviously she had been close to death plenty of times before, but this had been different. Dying by a gunshot to the head was a very human way of almost dying. To Kathy, it was more terrifying than any magical dangers she had ever faced.

She sighed and rested her head against the table to try to steady her shaky hands. Eyes closed, she concentrated on fighting the urge to fall asleep. She wondered how Samantha was doing and hoped that she hadn't had the baby yet. Kathy didn't want to miss that.

The door swung open and she shot upright.

"I'm sorry," Detective O'Leary said as she closed the door behind her. "Were you sleeping?"

Kathy shook her head. "No, it's okay."

The detective took a seat across the table from her.

"When can I see my sister?"

"Soon," O'Leary said. "I just wanted to chat with you privately before I let you go."

"Privately?" Kathy wondered how much of hers and Dennis' conversation O'Leary had heard before she fired her gun. She braced herself for any intruding questions.

"Off the record," the detective clarified. "We already have your statement, so that's all set officially. I just wanted to talk to you…" She trailed off, then let out a deep breath. "I couldn't help but overhear what you and Dennis were talking about…"

Kathy gulped, clawing desperately at the corners of her mind to recall exactly what she had discussed with Dennis. She knew they had talked about what happened last Halloween, but did she implicate herself as a witch? Did she admit to casting spells? In the trauma that had been nearly dying, she couldn't remember the specifics. Panic took over.

"That was—he had a gun to my head," she sputtered. "I was just saying whatever he wanted to hear."

"Oh." O'Leary looked a little disappointed. "So there wasn't any truth to what you said?"

They were both dancing around the topic, neither of them wanting to say it out loud for two very different fears: sounding stupid and being persecuted.

"Um…"

"*Was* there any truth to what you said to him, Miss Walker?"

Kathy closed her eyes and sighed. If she lied, and O'Leary really wanted to know what had happened, the detective could find out. Best to be honest from the start, especially if the conversation was truly "off the record."

"Yes, it's true."

Silence followed, stretching so long that Kathy looked up to make sure the detective hadn't dozed off herself.

"I'm not sure if you remember, but I was assigned to that Halloween case last year," O'Leary said. "I believe I was the one who interviewed you. It's a little hard to remember because I talked to so many people and it was quite a while ago."

"I remember." Kathy's voice was quiet, cautious.

O'Leary offered a brief smile. "Well, I'm sure you can imagine the mess we walked into. Officially, we put the case to rest, but there were still a lot of unexplained details. As a detective, that nags at me. I don't like leaving things unexplained."

Kathy didn't say anything when O'Leary paused. She wasn't sure where the conversation was going.

"Anyway, I guess I always somewhat knew that there was more to the story than what we were led to believe that night," the detective went on. "Something…" She trailed off then shook her head. "Never mind. I'm not going to say it. All I'm going to do is ask you one question. That night, in the basement of that house, you and your sister were able to stop that psycho for good?"

Stunned, Kathy simply nodded.

O'Leary leaned back in her chair and let out another sigh. "Good. I'm not even going to ask anymore questions. God knows I've seen enough evil in this world to know that it exists. No matter what you and your sister are or how you stopped that…*thing* that night, it's good to know that there's a source of unexplained good in the world too."

"Thank you."

"Don't mention it." The detective rose to her feet. "And just so we're clear, this conversation never happened. That goes both ways, okay?"

Again, Kathy nodded.

O'Leary started to the door, then stopped and looked back at Kathy. "Is your sister really having a baby?"

"Yeah, if she hasn't already. It's been a while since I've been able to check in on her."

"Well, we better get you up to see her then. No charges are being filed against you, Miss Walker. I'm the one who took the shots. They'll be investigating me, not you. And I'll keep your secret. Whatever it is."

"Thank you," Kathy said again.

They both smiled at each other, then O'Leary nodded to the door. "Come on. You don't want to miss your sister having a baby. Trust me, I was late for my nephew's birth and I haven't been able to live it down ever since."

With another smile, Kathy rose to her feet and followed the detective out the door.

CHAPTER 42

Kathy followed Detective O'Leary through the main lobby toward the elevators. Somehow, they had brought her up to the ground floor without Kathy even realizing it. She had been in such a daze—still was, a bit—that she hadn't paid much attention to her surroundings right after what had happened in the morgue.

The lobby, which had been nearly empty when Kathy had followed Dennis to the basement, was now packed with police officers, nurses, paramedics, reporters, and onlookers. The young witch kept her head low as she passed through the crowd, only looking up when she heard someone familiar shouting her name.

"Kathy!"

They were near the elevators. O'Leary had already pressed the call button for them. But Kathy stopped and looked into the crowd, her eyes almost immediately settling on Michael.

She approached him, giving a nod to the security officer who was trying to keep the crowd at bay. Taking Michael's hand, she led him around the corner away from the crowd. She waved at Detective O'Leary on her way. O'Leary smiled, then began helping the security officer control the crowd.

Kathy and Michael found a spot in the nook where the vending machines were. They could still hear the crowd behind them, but at least they had a little bit more privacy.

"Are you okay?" He wrapped her in a hug, squeezing tight and then pulled away to look at her. "I heard on the news what happened and I came as quick as I could."

Judging by the plaid pajama bottoms, that was entirely true. Night Number Two of seeing each other's bedclothes.

"I'm okay," she said with a nod. Whether it was to convince him or herself, she still wasn't clear on. But the truth was, she *was* okay. Nothing had happened, other than a close call. "But I'm glad you're here."

The hint of a smile curled on his lips before he decided better of it and went straight-faced. "You are?"

"Yeah." She pulled her arms behind her head and collected her hair and pulled it to the side. "I, uh…we need to talk about…what we talked about." She let out a nervous chuckle. "Earlier today, that is."

"You've had a long day. We can talk about it later. I'm just glad that you're okay." He moved to pull her in for another hug, but she pushed him away.

"No. I need to say this now." She took a deep breath and met his eyes. "What just happened to me was terrifying. Arguably the scariest thing I've ever faced in my life."

"Well yeah—"

She put up her hand. "Please. Let me finish."

He nodded for her to go ahead.

"What just happened…it helped me see what I had already known but was too scared to admit." She shook her head. "We can't be together, Michael. It just wouldn't be fair to you."

"What do you mean?"

"I'm not one hundred percent happy with my life right now," she admitted. "I'm getting there, but I just—I need to figure things out for a bit. On my own. I can't keep falling into these same patterns I have been. Going from relationship to relationship, hoping that the next one will be different. The truth is, I'm the problem in all of them."

"No. Don't say that. That's not true at all."

"How? I'm the common denominator in all of my failed relationships. *Of course* there were other issues too, but that doesn't make me any less of the problem." She let out another breath of air. "I need to be by myself for a while. Figure out who I am without a guy so I know what to look for with the next one. And I don't want to string you along while I'm going through that."

Michael ran his hand up and down her arm. "I can't say that I'm happy with that idea, but I can see where you're coming from. If you need to be alone, then that's my answer."

"I'm sorry."

"Don't be. You need to take care of yourself first. I'll be okay. I mean, it's not like we can't still be friends, right?"

Kathy offered a sad smile. "Right." But even as the word left her lips, she knew it was a lie. How often had she seen Michael since she and Jeremy had broken up? Their friendship was not strong enough to exist on its own without Jeremy or some other force pushing them together.

She hooked her thumb behind her toward the elevators. "I should go. Hopefully Samantha hasn't had the baby yet."

Michael hugged her again, squeezing tighter than he had before. In her ear, he said, "If you ever need anything, give me a call."

"I will."

When they parted, she could feel the tears burning her eyes, but she held her composure until she was alone on the elevator. Michael was a great friend and he may have possibly been a great partner in life. But she was never going to know for sure.

CHAPTER 43

When Kathy stepped off the elevator, she could see commotion around Samantha's hospital room.

"What's going on?" she asked Marty and Mary, who were in the waiting room.

"Samantha's in labor," Marty said.

"They wouldn't let us stay," Mary added, clearly annoyed. "Where have you been?"

Kathy ignored her and walked right up to Samantha's room, but was stopped by a nurse who stood in the doorway.

"Ma'am, I need you to stand back," she said, pressing a firm hand against Kathy's shoulder.

"But that's my sister!" Kathy said.

"Kathy!" Samantha called from inside the room. "Let her in!"

"Only the father is allowed in the room during delivery," the nurse said to Samantha.

"I don't care! Let her in!"

The nurse looked between the sisters, then turned to the doctor. He was seated at the end of the bed. He nodded and waved Kathy in.

"Shut the door," he told the nurse.

"If you're going to be in here," the nurse said, "you need to suit up like the rest of us." She offered Kathy a blue overall suit, which Kathy quickly slipped on.

Samantha squeezed Kathy's hand tight when she made it to her side next to Steven. "I was afraid you were going to miss it. Is everything okay?"

Kathy nodded, tearful that this moment had finally come. "Everything's taken care of."

Steven put an arm around Kathy. "Thank you."

"All right, Mrs. Harper," the doctor said. "We're going to need you to start pushing now."

Samantha gripped her husband's hand like a vice while Kathy stroked the hair out of her eyes and offered encouraging words.

And for as long as it took to get to that moment, the delivery went surprisingly quick.

Before long, Samantha held her newborn baby boy in her arms as tears streamed down her face. Steven's eyes were misty as well. Kathy stood by and smiled at the new family, an immense sense of happiness flowing through her.

The doctors and nurses finished up their tasks, but left the room afterward to give them some alone time.

After a moment, Kathy came to her senses. "Oh! I brought a camera with me! We need to get a picture of the three of you!"

Turning, she found her bag perched beside the chair she and Steven had taken turns sitting in all day. Retrieving the disposable camera, she raised it to her eyes, squeezed the other eye shut, and said, "Smile!"

With a flash, the camera flicked and she cranked the turnstile to ready the next picture.

"Have you thought of a name yet?" Kathy asked.

"We have," Samantha said with a smile.

"And?"

"This is Joshua Harper."

"Oh! Little Baby Josh!" Kathy cooed. "I love it!"

Samantha and Steven both beamed with pride at their son. Kathy watched them and was sure that she had made the right decision with Michael. If she was ever going to have a moment like this one, things needed to change in her life. That meant being on her own for a while.

Although, now that there was a new baby, she knew she'd be back at the house all the time to see Little Baby Josh.

Kathy and her sister, Samantha, have always been a team. Throughout their time as witches, they've taken out more than their share of bad guys. But after Kathy meets Will, who she learns is a demonic Dark Knight, her loyalties begin to change.

Meanwhile, Samantha doesn't trust Will or his intentions. Still, Kathy can't help but feel tempted by the dark side as she falls deeper in love with Will. Crossing over would give Kathy the freedom to do whatever she wanted with her magic. No rules. No limitations. It would also mean breaking the bond she has always shared with her sister, who has made it clear that she wants nothing to do with the dark side.

When Will proposes they take over the underworld, Kathy loves the idea of having power. But it also leaves her with a choice that will change her life: abandon her family and the life she has always known, or give up the love of her life forever.

THE FULL MOON

UNDER THE MOON: BOOK 1

Read on for an excerpt of the first book in
the Under the Moon series, a sequel series
to the Coven series!

DAVID NETH

CHAPTER 1

- APRIL 2005 -

"Hold the elevator!" Kathy raced through the lobby with her bag slung over her shoulder. She was trying not to trip in her heels.

The men and women in the crowded elevator ignored her, pretending to not see her racing through the lobby like a madwoman. Luckily, a man held out his hand in between the doors just as they were about to close. He was wearing a black suit that fit him perfectly. Kathy was surprised. It was a rare sight to see a man dressed so nicely. But then, she had never really gone to an office building like this before. Her prior experiences with men were the try-too-hard Abercrombie type. And she was definitely over those guys.

She was glad that she had at least one good suit of her own.

The Full Moon

It wasn't exactly a suit, but the gray between the jacket and the skirt matched so perfectly that nobody noticed. She checked out the other women in the elevator with her and judged how much they spent on their outfits. More money than she had, certainly.

"Thank you!" Kathy smiled and repositioned the bag on her shoulder. She hit the button for the fifth floor and squeezed in next to the man.

"Of course. I never mind sharing an elevator with a pretty lady like yourself." He smiled.

Kathy rolled her eyes and noticed how many other people did the same. He was certainly trying to charm her, but she would've been lying if she said it didn't help. Especially when she was already stressing out. She smiled at him briefly and then fixed her eyes on the display above the elevator doors that read which floor they were on. With the amount of people on the elevator, it was no surprise that it stopped at every floor. She grumbled at the people who got off on the second floor. Couldn't they take the stairs? The doors opened on the fourth floor and the man stepped out.

"I hope you have a wonderful day," he said as he exited the elevator.

Kathy smiled and muttered, "You too."

Soon she stepped out onto the fifth floor and searched for Johnson & Cramer, Inc.

The hallway was bland, nothing like the beautiful lobby on the first floor, with cream walls and no signs directing where each business was located. She stepped away from the elevator and decided to take a left, searching for the correct office. She reached the end of the hall and still hadn't found it so she turned, passed the elevator again, and went in the opposite direction, finally finding the place.

There wasn't anyone at the front desk, so she tapped the little bell on the counter and waited. Soon a man in a loose-fitting gray suit walked out of his office with a to-go cup of coffee from the café downstairs. His blazer gaped open and unbuttoned and his belly hung over his belt.

"You here for the interview?"

Kathy extended her hand with a smile—one she'd practiced with her sister the night before—and said, "Yes. I'm Kathy Walker. So nice to meet you. Are you Mr. Johnson or Mr. Cramer?"

The man chuckled. "No, they're both dead." Her face flushed with embarrassment, but she smiled and tried to play it off. The man shook Kathy's hand and then took a sip of his coffee. "I'm Richard Burke. I'm the sales manager. Why don't you come in my office and we can chat?"

Kathy nodded and followed him.

"Have a seat," he offered with an extended hand as he looped around to his seat behind his desk. Papers littered it, except for the area on the corner of the desk to his left where his computer sat. "I had a chance to take a look at your résumé." He sighed. "Honestly, I was a little underwhelmed. You have very little job experience. My concern is that if I hired you to be my assistant, you wouldn't be able to keep up with the work."

Kathy's stomach lurched. This guy cut right to the chase. "Yeah, I…um…well, I have been out of work for a bit, helping my sister raise her kids. She has two boys." Since Samantha's husband left her last month, she had been her sister's support at home. But now that Steven's paycheck wasn't coming in, Kathy needed to chip in financially, too.

Richard looked down at his copy of her résumé.

Her last job had been at the gas station. She worked the overnights and saw her fair share of weirdos. "Well, officially," she added as he scanned her résumé. "In that time I've been working under-the-table a bit."

Richard leaned back in his chair and rocked back and forth, his right leg crossed over his left. He balanced his coffee on his bent knee and held the foot resting on his knee with his free hand. "Yeah? What kind of work was that?"

Kathy hesitated. "I was working at a hotel downtown, occasionally."

"Front desk?" There was optimism in his voice.

"Um…actually, more in the entertainment…business." She saw his eyebrows scrunch together in confusion and pressed on. "They hired me as a psychic. Actually, in that position I was able to learn some great communication and customer service skills that I think would be useful to me at a job like this." She was hoping she could spin her desperate stint at the hotel into something positive.

Richard smiled. "Miss Walker, I appreciate your enthusiasm for this position, but I'm afraid you aren't qualified enough. I have interviews lined up with other applicants with years of experience working in a secretarial position who would make excellent assistants. I'm sorry, but I don't think this is going to work out."

Kathy gave him a curt smile and reached for her bag on the side of her chair. "Well, I appreciate you taking the time to meet with me. Good luck filling the position."

"Well, hold on a minute, Miss Walker," Richard said. He stood and walked to the door, closing it. "I believe I could free up some room on the payroll, if you'd be willing to do some…extracurricular work." He stepped closer to her and reached for her hand.

She backed away from him until she was up against the wall.

"You'd have the same salary, benefits, everything. I'm sure I could find something around here for you to do." He placed his hand on her hip and moved closer.

She put her hands on his chest and pushed him back. "Mr. Burke, I may be unqualified for this position, but I'm not stupid. I'm not going to be your office whore so you can feel like a man."

"Whoa, sweetie—"

"*Don't* call me 'sweetie.'" She moved to exit, but he grabbed her arm. "Let go of me, Mr. Burke."

"I'm sure we can sort something out," he pushed.

THE FULL MOON

Kathy whipped her arm around, breaking free of his hold. She held up her other hand, and he stopped moving, frozen in place. With a deep breath, she contemplated kicking him to prove her point but decided against it.

Instead, she opened the door and exited his office. One of the insurance agents by the front desk asked how the interview went.

"Your boss is a pervert," Kathy stated. She repositioned her bag, hooked her thumb on the strap, and walked to the elevator.

On her way down, the elevator stopped once more on the fourth floor and the man in the black suit stepped in.

"You know you can't live in the elevator, right?"

Kathy rolled her eyes and ignored him.

"Bad day?"

She nodded.

"Care to unload it on a complete stranger over lunch?"

She looked up at him. "Right now? Don't you have to work?" She had only been at the interview for fifteen minutes, max. Didn't this guy have anything better to do than ride the elevator all day?

He shrugged. "Yeah. Unless you have other plans."

Kathy wanted to say no, but she was not one to believe in coincidences. This was the second random encounter with this man today. It had to mean something. "Sure, all right."

"Yeah? Do you have a preference on a place to go? You seem like an easy-to-please girl."

Sidestepping his comment, Kathy suggested the café downstairs.

"Sounds good to me." He held out his hand. "I'm Will, by the way."

"Kathy." His grip was firm and his smile was charming, but she was sure this would be the last she saw of him. She had no intention of ever showing her face in this office building again.

They ordered at the counter, and the woman who helped them already had Will's dish ready to go when they arrived.

"I called from upstairs. This is my usual go-to place for lunch," he explained.

"Oh. Did you want to go somewhere else?" Kathy asked.

"No, I like it here."

After Kathy ordered, they took a seat at a table by the window.

"So do you care to spill about your lousy, horrible, no good, rotten day, or do you want me to help you forget about it?" Will asked.

Kathy smiled, stirring her spoon in her soup. "I had a job interview for an assistant position at Johnson & Cramer...basically a glorified secretary."

"I'm guessing it didn't go well?" Will took a bite of his wrap.

"Besides the fact that I have no relevant job experience and that I've essentially been unemployed for the last six years, the guy was a real dick," Kathy blurted. She sat back and took a deep breath. "Sorry."

Will held up his hands in a surrender gesture and said, "I know. Bad day."

"And now I have to go home and tell my sister that I screwed this up," she continued. She absently stirred her spoon in her soup. Being the hotel psychic wasn't really a lucrative job, but it helped. Now that the hotel was under new management, Kathy had been the first to go. Samantha had been nagging her since then to find another job.

"You're supposed to eat it," Will joked, indicating her soup. Kathy cracked a smile and let go of her spoon. "Look on the bright side: you were still able to walk out of there with your head held high. And hey, you still have your *incredibly* good looks."

"Apparently that's all I'm good for." She turned her attention out the window at the crowd walking on the sidewalk. They had jobs and families and places to be. For a moment, Kathy envied them.

Will wiped his hands and looked at her. "That's not what I meant…"

"I know. But that's what Richard Burke was looking for. Some office fun," Kathy said. "I'm sorry. I shouldn't be telling you all this. You work in the same building as him."

"Richard Burke?"

Kathy nodded.

"That man is a snake! His last secretary left after suing him for sexual harassment! If I knew you were going there, I would've warned you!" He tossed his napkin on the table. "I'm going to straighten him out."

"No! I already took care of it." She wondered if her magic still had its hold on him. She didn't want Will walking in on a magically frozen Burke. Even if she planned on never seeing him again.

"You're right." Will relaxed. "You don't need anyone to fight your battles for you. You certainly look like you can take care of yourself. But please, eat."

Kathy smiled and brought a spoonful to her mouth. Her first bite to eat since breakfast. "Wow, this is good!"

He smiled. "Right? That's why it's my daily favorite."

She ate a bit more and asked, "So where do you work?"

"I actually am in charge of a small law firm up on the fourth floor. William Brown Attorneys."

"Wow! That's incredible!"

"Yeah, it's pretty nice being my own boss and all. Right now it's just me and another lawyer friend of mine, so a lot of the housekeeping stuff like finances, phone calls, meetings, they're all done by me. Well, pretty much."

"Are you looking for a secretary?" Kathy smiled.

"Do you know someone?"

"Maybe." Kathy broke up some crackers in what was left of her soup.

"I know who you're talking about. I heard she's completely unqualified." He smiled.

"Too soon!" Kathy laughed and tossed a bit of her cracker at him.

He put his hands up in another surrender gesture and said, "I'm kidding. But really, I would love to hire you, but the money just isn't there yet. Hopefully soon. I'll definitely keep my eyes open for you, though."

"How are you going to reach me if you find something?" Kathy took a spoonful of the rest of her soup. As thick as he was laying it on, she was surprised he hadn't weaseled her number out of her sooner.

"I was hoping this would be a sly way to get your number."

"You think it's that easy, huh?" Kathy laughed.

"Well, I did buy you lunch," Will prodded, flashing a smile. "And I've been a shoulder to cry on in this devastating time of your life."

Kathy rolled her eyes again. "Oh, what a gentleman. Do you have a pen?"

"Of course." He opened his jacket and pulled a gold ballpoint pen out of the inside pocket. It had the name of his business branded on the side.

"You can't afford a secretary, but you can buy novelty pens?" Kathy scribbled her name and number on a fresh napkin. She couldn't believe she was doing this. The last time she'd given a guy a number like this she had been drunk. She'd needed to change her number in order to get him and his buddies to stop calling.

"It's called *branding*. Some expenses are worth it," Will explained. "Plus, I can write it off."

Kathy smiled and slid the napkin over to him. "Don't give this to your college buddies for a late-night booty call. I have caller ID."

Will folded it and placed it in the pocket inside his jacket. He placed his hand over it and declared, "I will protect this to the death."

Kathy laughed. Her day was turning out to be better than where it was originally heading.

Will glanced at his watch. "Oooh, I have to go. I have a meeting with a client in half an hour and I haven't prepared for it yet. Can I walk you to your car?"

Kathy cringed. Her best self was not coming across. "I don't have a car, actually. You could walk me to the bus station, but it's about three blocks away."

"Where do you live?"

"Just on the edge of the city on Arlington. Not exactly easy walking, especially in these shoes." Kathy stuck out her foot so Will could see the artificial height she was walking on.

"I see that." He stood and offered his hand to help her up. "I will walk you to the bus stop, but I'm afraid I won't be able to wait with you."

Kathy took his hand and stood. For a moment they were nearly pressed up against each other until Will took a step back. "Won't you be late for your meeting?"

"I'm my own boss, remember? I think it's worth it. I want to make sure your day only gets better from here."

"You're really working it, huh?" Kathy said, leading him out of the café and in the direction of the bus stop.

"Is it working?"

"Maybe you should try that number to find out," Kathy suggested. They crossed the intersection and she reached for her ear. "I think I lost an earring."

Will looked around the sidewalk. "I'll check the other side."

She grabbed his arm to stop him and said, "It's not a big deal. I have more."

When they reached the bus stop, they both hesitated, unsure how to properly say good-bye.

"Thank you for lunch."

"It was my pleasure," Will said. "Good luck on your job search, and I will definitely be keeping my eye open for you."

Will moved to kiss her cheek and ran into Kathy's extended hand. They laughed and settled on a wave.

Kathy watched as Will walked back to the office building. She couldn't help but smile. All things considered, it was a very good day.

CHAPTER 2

Kathy gulped down a glass of water after her morning run. She had taken her nephews to school and had already thrown in a load of laundry. Her goal for the day was to set up a couple more job interviews. Her sister, Samantha, had helped her tweak her résumé to make it look more professional. Kathy hoped the changes would do the trick. She also hoped that she never met another interviewer like Richard Burke, but she knew that was likely a fantasy.

She grabbed a hand towel from the stove and wiped away the sweat beading up on her forehead. She had just kicked off her sneakers when the doorbell rang.

Kathy peered through the stained glass on the front door, trying to make out who it was. It was not unusual to get unexpected or uninvited guests. She relaxed a bit when she saw a suit coat and tie. Anything that was looking to kill her or her family was not usually dressed so nicely.

"Good morning." It was Will. Kathy flashed him a smile and then realized that she looked like a mess. A complete opposite of what she'd looked like the last time she'd seen him. Instead of a gray pinstripe suit coat and skirt, she wore a pink tank top and black shorts. Her hair was matted with sweat, and she was sure she stank, too.

"Hi," Kathy responded, a little confused. "How do you know where I live?"

"You told me Arlington, remember?"

She ran her hand along the top of her head, hoping to smooth out a few escaped hairs from her ponytail. It still didn't make sense. She had only met Will once and here he was on her doorstep.

Finally, Will sighed. "Okay, I cheated. I asked a neighbor. Told her you were a friend of mine from college."

Kathy pointed to the house across the street. "Mrs. Kors?" Kathy's busybody neighbor was always looking for reasons to check in or get the latest gossip. As a retired woman in her 70s, she frequently binged on the latest scoop.

"The short old woman across the street?" He tossed a thumb behind him. "She seemed sweet."

"That's the one." She folded her arms across her chest and asked, "So…what are you doing here?"

"Well I bought you lunch last week, I just figured it was your turn to return the favor." He flashed another charming smile. Kathy cocked an eyebrow. "I'm kidding, unless you're offering." He paused to see if she would bite. When she didn't, he continued, "What I came here for was to return this." He held out his hand. Sitting in the middle of his palm was the earring Kathy had lost the day of her interview.

"Where'd you find it?" She scooped it up and studied it, making sure it was the same one.

"One of the girls at the café found it. They thought it might belong to you since it was at my usual seat," Will explained.

"Well, it was very nice of you to return it. Thank you," Kathy said. She gripped the door and made to close it, but Will's voice stopped her.

"Would you like to go to dinner sometime?"

Kathy stopped and looked at him before answering. Her knee-jerk reaction was to say no. She knew she wasn't exactly a catch. Unemployed and living with her sister, who was a single mother of two. The only thing going for her was her looks, and she knew that whenever a guy spontaneously asked her out, he was rarely looking for a meaningful relationship. However, the more she looked at Will, the more she found herself forgetting all her previous experience with men.

"On a date?"

Will tilted his head sideways and nodded shyly. "I was hoping."

THE FULL MOON

They considered each other for a moment. A crash from the kitchen broke Kathy's trance. She knew her sister wouldn't be home all day, and it was too early for the boys.

"Um…sure, yeah, I will." She looked back into the house and then back at Will. She needed to get rid of him, fast. The noise was likely an attack, and she didn't want Will caught in the crossfire, nor did she want her secret exposed.

"Is everything all right?" He stepped forward, but Kathy pushed him away.

"Yeah, it's fine. Look, you have my number, so call me and we'll set something up." She closed the door farther and farther as she spoke. "Bye!"

Once the door was shut, she raced to the kitchen. She saw a puddle of water by the sink but no sign of an intruder. Grabbing a knife, she crept through the house. She stopped when she stepped in another puddle of water in the living room, which soaked into her socks. Looking around on the floor for a trail of water to indicate where the trespasser was, she tensed up when she felt a drop of water on her neck. She looked up and gasped.

A slimy fishlike creature perched upside down on the vaulted ceiling. Covered in scales and fins lining the middle of his head and down his back, he bared his razor-sharp teeth and hissed when Kathy spotted him. His long claws dug into the wall, holding him in place.

After a moment of hesitation, he lunged at Kathy. She slipped on the puddle as she tried to escape and fell to the ground. The creature caught her ankle in his slimy grasp and pulled her toward him. Kathy managed to grab on to the front parlor door frame and used her other foot to swing around and kick the beast in the face.

Back on her feet, she snatched up the knife and drove it into the creature's chest. Despite being impaled, the creature let out a roar and swatted at Kathy, scratching her arm and drawing blood.

She scrambled up the stairs and to her bedroom, slamming the door behind her. She searched for something she could use to contain him or slow him down.

Kicking open the door, the creature hissed once again at Kathy before stepping into the room. Out of options, she nabbed her hair dryer, and firing it up to full blast, she pointed it at the creature. He sent out another hiss and jumped out of the hallway window and down to the yard. Kathy watched as he jumped over the fence and down the street. She swore to herself, knowing there was no way she would be able to catch him on her own.

* * *

I'm home!" Samantha announced as she walked through the front door.

"We're in the kitchen!" Kathy called. She was pulling a pan out of the oven. "And dinner's ready!" It was a chicken left over from another meal that Samantha had made a few weeks before. All Kathy needed to do was pull it out of the freezer and stick it in the oven.

"Oooh, perfect timing!" Samantha hooked her keys by the door and kissed each of her boys on the head. They were at the kitchen table doing homework. Sixteen-year-old Josh, Samantha's oldest, was the main reason his brother, Chris, who was fourteen, finished any of his homework at all. "How was your day, boys?"

"Good," they droned.

Once the table was cleared of textbooks and notebooks, Kathy, Samantha, and the boys sat down for dinner.

"Any luck with your job hunt?" Samantha asked her sister. She cut into her chicken and took a bite.

"Y'know, I started the day off great. Very productive, but some things happened and it just didn't turn out," Kathy said. She knew Samantha didn't like to talk about demonic attacks too much in front of the boys. The attacks were inevitable, but Samantha wanted her children to be as normal as possible without being scarred by whatever was hiding in their closets.

Kathy thought the whole idea was stupid. The boys would need to know how to use their magic to protect themselves eventually. It was only a matter of time before they were targeted. But they were Samantha's kids, so Kathy tried to keep talk of demonic activity to a minimum.

As a result, the sisters often used ridiculous excuses to evade any magic talk. Kathy was sure the boys didn't buy it, though. Josh and Chris were young, not stupid. They were smarter than Samantha sometimes gave them credit for.

"I noticed the laundry didn't get done," Samantha pressed.

"But I mopped the floor," Kathy countered.

"And she made dinner," Josh added. The sisters bickered a lot, especially now that Kathy wasn't bringing in any money. Josh remembered how much arguing there was in the house when his dad was still around. So now he always tried to calm the storm before it turned into something bigger.

Hearing her son's tone, Samantha gave in. "Yes, you're right. Thank you, Kathy." She turned to her youngest son and asked, "Did you finish your homework?"

"I just have a couple of math problems left, but they shouldn't take me long," Chris said. He attempted to shove a giant spoonful of mashed potatoes in his mouth.

"Smaller bites, Chris, c'mon," Samantha said. She thought back to the days when their father had been there to help her out. It made her sad to think that Steven could so easily abandon his family. His children.

When dinner was over, Samantha and Kathy started on the dishes as the boys finished their homework.

"There was an attack today," Kathy whispered to her sister. "And I didn't get him."

Samantha put down the plate she was drying and turned to Josh and Chris.

THE FULL MOON

"Boys, would you mind finishing upstairs in your room? Your aunt and I need to discuss some stuff," Samantha said.

"Are you going to talk about magic? I want to help!" Chris loved magic, despite not having any active powers of his own.

Samantha tried not to lie to the boys, so it was difficult for her to respond truthfully when they asked her outright about magic. "Yes, we are. But right now I need you to finish your homework." She smiled at him. "We'll come to you guys if we need help."

Chris sighed and left the room with Josh. Samantha knew the boys—especially Chris—were anxious to be in the midst of the action, but it would be too soon before they were. She wanted to protect them as long as she could, but she also needed to prepare them for any attack that might happen if she or Kathy wasn't around. Now that they were getting older, it was getting harder and harder to keep them in someone's company for their protection.

Once the boys were gone, Samantha pressed Kathy for more details. Her sister dried her hands and pulled the magic book out from the pantry.

"I was looking through it when the boys came home," Kathy explained. "I really don't think we should hide it from them this much. They should know that at any minute we could be attacked."

"I don't want them to be terrified their whole lives. They're just kids," Samantha said.

"They're teenagers, they're not helpless," Kathy countered. She flipped to a page in the book. "Anyway, this is the guy who attacked me."

"Vepar?"

Kathy nodded and pointed to a warning in the entry. "This scared me."

Samantha read from the book: "'If his blood mixes with anyone else's, they too will become a creature like him.' Did he bleed on you?"

Kathy shook her head. "No, but he scratched me pretty good." She showed off her wounded arm. "His blood didn't mix with mine, but I got some of his slime in there. I thought that might add to the mutation process, but I think I'm good."

"Why didn't you call me?" Samantha gripped her sister's elbow and examined her arm. "What would've happened if the boys came home and you were some fish-mutant?"

"Plus side? I'm not. And the book has a potion that'll help kill him," Kathy said.

"Okay." Samantha let go of Kathy's arm and looked at the entry in the book. "So do you have anything of his that we can track him with?"

Kathy bit her lip. "No. I didn't think of it. I mopped up the mess so the boys wouldn't see, and that was all he had leftover. But he freaked out when I shot my hair dryer at him, so I'm guessing he can't stay out of the water that long."

"Kathy! It's going to be impossible to find him!"

"Why? I just figured he'd be in the lake. We head out to Presque Isle and look for him. Simple as that. He'll probably want to stay away from people, so a beach in April is perfect."

Samantha tucked her dark hair behind both of her ears and crossed her arms. The same stance she took whenever the boys were making poor arguments to get out of housework and she was getting frustrated with them. Kathy didn't appreciate Samantha treating her like one of the kids.

"Think about it, Kathy. Do you know how many people in Erie have a swimming pool? By April they still have them closed, which means they're not using them. Not to mention that it rains a lot this time of year, so he could probably rehydrate himself without entering a large body of water. And what about if he hurts someone before we can find him?"

Kathy held up her hands. "All very good points. But look, I actually saw this thing with my own eyes. He's not that intelligent. Someone sent him. He's not going to hurt anybody unless whoever is in charge of him orders him to do it. Since he came here looking for me, I'm most likely the target."

Samantha sighed and leaned back on the counter. "Okay. But I still think it's a good idea to equip every one of us—including the boys—with this potion so that, just in case you're not the sole target, we are all protected."

Kathy smirked. "You're going to corrupt the minds of your tiny children? How will they survive!?" She laughed and Samantha shot her a look.

"Finish the dishes. I'll start heating water."

They began preparing the potion, dropping in the various ingredients the book called for. They only had to substitute a few, but Samantha was very confident in her potion-making abilities and knew the substitutions wouldn't be a problem.

"So why do you think you're the target?" Samantha asked. She was waiting for the potion to thicken before adding the next ingredient.

Kathy shrugged and continued with the dishes. "I don't know. Maybe it's the whole family? I was just the only one home. I know several people are dying to get their hands on the book. Or it could be our powers. You never know with these things."

"True. Which is why we need to be extra careful. We don't know enough about this guy," Samantha said.

"Yeah, but I don't think we should put our lives on hold just because we get attacked." Kathy set a dish in the drying rack. "We should still go to work, go shopping, go on dates, see friends…you know…"

Samantha raised her eyebrows and smiled. "Do you have something you want to tell me?"

She could always tell when Kathy was seeing someone new. She acted like a teenager every time she was about to go on a first date. Still, it had been a while since Kathy was this lovesick. She began giving up on men once she saw the pain Steven had inflicted on Samantha when he left. Samantha was glad to see that Kathy was getting over her fear of getting hurt like she did.

THE FULL MOON

Kathy shrugged. "Last week when I was at that crappy job interview, this guy I met in the elevator asked me to lunch—"

"You meet guys in the most random places!"

"I wasn't putting out! It was just lunch!" Kathy was smiling. A week had passed since she'd first met Will Brown, and she barely thought of him. Now she couldn't help smiling whenever she did. "Anyway, he showed up this morning and asked me out."

"House call?"

"I lost an earring." Kathy knew what her sister was implying.

Samantha smiled and added the next ingredient. "All right, this thing is just about done. Let me go warn the boys."

"They'll be fine, Sammy. Don't worry about it too much."

CHAPTER 3

Kathy's phone buzzed on the table for the third time that morning.

"Are you ever going to answer that?" Chris asked. He was lifting the bowl of sugary milk leftover from his cereal to his mouth.

Kathy silenced her phone. "I know what he's calling for, and I don't have an answer yet."

"Is it your lawyer?" Samantha was spreading butter on a bagel.

Kathy rolled her eyes and smiled. "He's not *mine*. But yeah, it's him."

"Have you gone out yet?" Samantha asked.

Kathy shook her head. "Not yet."

The Full Moon

Josh held a piece of toast between his teeth and slid his books into his backpack. When his hand was free, he took a bite and asked, "What are you waiting for?"

"With Vepar attacking at any minute, I don't want to risk bringing someone home and exposing our secret. Or accidentally getting him killed," Kathy explained. Samantha shot her a look so she added, "Not that anyone's dying. We just have to be careful, that's all."

Samantha was eager to change the subject. "Do you boys have your potions?"

Chris waved it in the air. "Got it!" He slipped it into his pocket.

"Don't get it taken away this time, okay? I used the last of the mugwort in that batch." The last time the boys had needed to take a potion to school, Chris kept playing with it in class and it had been confiscated by the teacher. That had been a tough one to explain.

"All right, get your things." She shot a glance at the clock. "Oooh, I didn't realize it was so late already. We need to go." She popped the last bite of her bagel in her mouth, wiped her hands on her napkin, and rushed out the door with Josh and Chris in tow.

When her sister and her nephews shuffled out of the house, Kathy stood from her seat to tackle the dishes. Just as she filled the sink, her phone rang again.

It was Will. Again. She stared at it for a moment, deciding

whether or not she should answer it. She wanted to go out with him, but she didn't know how to tell him that she was putting off their date on account of his safety. She didn't want to give him the impression that she was blowing him off. After going back and forth in her mind, she finally dried her hands and answered at the last second.

"I'm so sorry I haven't gotten back to you," Kathy started before he could say anything.

"Are you even still interested? I asked you out a week ago, and I haven't spoken to you since. I thought I might've had the wrong number." His deep, warm voice was a very nice sound to hear that early in the morning. Kathy couldn't help but smile and wonder what was wrong with her.

She cringed and tried to keep a casual tone. "Yeah, sorry. It's been a crazy week. But my nights are basically free the rest of this week." As long as Samantha was home to watch the boys, she wouldn't have to worry too much about an attack from Vepar. Her sister would definitely call if something happened. They each had the potion, so all that they needed to do was wait it out. There hadn't been any strange reports, so obviously Vepar wasn't on a killing spree.

"How's tonight?"

"Tonight?" Her voice betrayed her with a squeak. She cleared it and said, "Um…yeah, that could work."

"I hope you're in the mood for seafood. There's this great restaurant at the hotel on the bay," Will said.

THE FULL MOON

Kathy's mind snapped to her intermittent stints as the hotel psychic. She knew that hotel—and that restaurant—*very* well. Showing her face there would be embarrassing, but she didn't want to tell him no again. "Perfect."

"Great! I'll pick you up at six?"

"You already know where I live, so sounds good."

* * *

As Will and Kathy walked into the hotel, he apologized for having to park so far away. There was an event at the convention center on the next pier over, taking up all the area parking. They'd managed to find street parking but still ended up walking six blocks.

"Will, it's fine. It's not your fault." She wore a sleeveless red satin dress with black heels. By the time they reached the hotel, her feet were happy to be resting. They were certainly not hiking shoes.

Will ordered for the two of them. Kathy didn't hear what it was he ordered—for dinner or for wine. When he saw her concerned face, he said, "You'll like it. Trust me."

She smiled and took a sip of her water. "So, how's the practice?"

"Good, actually. I signed another client just today. Her case doesn't seem to be too hard, but I guess we'll see what the defense has when we get to court," he said. "How's the job hunt?"

"Horrible." She took another sip of her water nervously. The fancy hotel with seafood and wine, it was not her typical style. These weren't her type of people. She felt like a fake for trying to be like them. She usually set up in the front lobby, dressed in her most festive psychic attire and asking folks if they'd like to know their future. She set her glass on the table and took a deep breath. "Have you heard of any openings for me?"

"You see, I realized later that I don't know much about you," he said with a smile. "I'd like to change that."

Kathy looked him in the eyes. She liked him. He had potential, that much she knew, but she wanted to be sure he understood just what he was getting into. From what she could tell, Will was used to elegant seafood dinners. The piano playing softly in the corner didn't strike him as too much. Kathy was used to heating up ramen in the microwave and watching TV while slurping up her noodles on the couch. She needed to set the record straight before either of them got in too deep. "Actually, my last job was at this hotel."

"Oh, really? Front desk?"

She smiled briefly and said, "Hotel psychic. I wasn't exactly on the payroll, but they let me set up a table. I made decent money, too. But then the hotel staff thought I was taking away customers from their other services and they asked me to leave." Waiting for his reaction, she took another sip of water and asked, "Your thoughts?"

He seemed confused, but not scared like Kathy expected.

He smoothed out the cloth napkin on his lap. "Can't say I've ever heard that one before. It's interesting."

"Most people thought I was nuts. Especially since I didn't have a car, so I took the bus. To most of the city I was the crazy psychic lady. I'm surprised you've never heard of me." That was a lie. People on the bus definitely gave her quizzical looks, but she didn't have the reputation. At least, not to her knowledge.

"What was your niche? Tarot cards, palm readings, crystal balls?"

Kathy smiled. No one who didn't have at least a little knowledge about mediums ever asked about her niche. He was more interesting than she'd given him credit for. But there was still more left to tell—a lot more. If only he knew just how divine she was.

"I've never done tarot cards. I couldn't tell you how to read them. And if a psychic has a crystal ball at her table, run. She's a scammer. I mostly did palm readings. Occasionally, I did tea leaves as well, but the hotel didn't really like it when I brought in a dump bucket for the water."

"Could you read my palm?" He offered his hand, and she took it before she realized what she'd just agreed to. A lot of times she had an actual vision—an extension of her time specialty as a witch. She wondered if she would be able to see his future on command. Sometimes it was difficult to determine the difference between the reading and her feelings.

She forced herself to look down at his hand. Tracing some

of the wrinkles in his palm, she shared her findings. "Well, I see lots of stress…likely from your start-up. Conflict…passion…oh, but then here's success." She pointed a finger to a spot on his palm. "See that line? That's what's to come. This over here," she moved her finger, "that's what is."

"Can you see what was?" He looked up at her, and she realized they had been leaning closer to each other.

She sat back and reached for her water again. She opened her mouth to respond but was interrupted by the waitress bringing over the wine. Kathy breathed a sigh of relief. They were only twenty minutes into their first date and she was already searching his palms, hoping to see their futures connected. She needed to cool down.

"What do you think?" Will held up his wineglass.

Kathy took a sip and considered for a moment. It was rich. Full bodied with a hint of strawberry. She didn't know much about wine, but she knew this was good. "Very nice."

"It's only half as good as the food." He brought the glass to his lips but pulled it away before taking a sip. He raised it in front of him instead. "To a wonderful evening with a beautiful woman. How did I get so lucky?"

"Don't get too excited about that success in your future." She raised her glass and clinked it with his before taking another sip.

* * *

THE FULL MOON

After dinner, the two walked hand-in-hand to the end of the pier. The evening had gone perfectly. Kathy hadn't enjoyed a date so much in a while. She could already tell that things were different with Will.

The full moon was out, reflecting off Lake Erie and illuminating the sky. The glow from the city lights helped brighten the sky as well.

"It's beautiful," Kathy said. She rested her head against his arm.

"I like to come out here every so often just for the view. Presque Isle has an even better view, but—"

"I think this is perfect." She looked up at him and reached up on her toes to meet his lips. Kathy knew from his kiss that falling for him was a good thing—a great thing.

Prior to meeting Will, she'd felt completely burnt out from all the stress in her life: making a living with no skills an employer would be interested in, helping her sister raise Josh and Chris, and keeping up with her supernatural responsibilities was a bit too much at times. But standing out on the edge of the pier with Will completely erased all that, and for the first time in a long time, she was carelessly happy. All her subconscious thoughts were gone, and she was entirely in the moment.

The two were so consumed with each other that they didn't hear the splashing of the water. It wasn't until Kathy felt a slimy hand on her leg that her attention was brought back to reality.

She landed with a thud on the pier as something pulled her into the water. The water was up to her waist by the time Will had hold of both of her arms and pulled her up. The splash of the water hid the creature from sight, which Kathy was grateful for. She didn't want Will to see. She might be able to still pass this off as her being clumsy.

Once she was safely on deck, Will asked if she was all right. She barely had time to nod before Vepar lunged from the water and landed on the edge of the pier. He hissed at the couple, spraying them with water and slime.

Kathy put her hands up and froze both Vepar and Will. She needed to act quickly. She knew there would likely have been people in the hotel or farther down the pier who had seen or heard the commotion. She searched for her purse that held the potion to kill the water creature, but she couldn't find it. She must've dropped it in the water when he first pulled her in.

She needed to get Will away safely without exposing who she was. If that was even still possible. She could easily have unfrozen him and ran, but then she would be facing twenty questions about what happened. She wasn't ready for that conversation with him yet.

Before she could think of anything, her magic wore off and both Will and Vepar unfroze. The creature swiped at Will with his claws, tearing his blazer. Kathy pulled off her shoes and drove a heel into the creature's back. She saw the point of the knife she'd stabbed him with the week before and knew it wouldn't stop him. He turned and pushed her. Landing on the edge of the pier, she moved to get up, but when she shifted her weight she lost her balance and began to topple into the dark water. She gripped the bollard on the edge of the pier to keep herself from falling in.

Looking up at Will, she saw him charge Vepar, and a large sword appeared in his hands. Swinging it sideways, he tore through the creature's flesh and its head dropped to the dock. He kept swinging until pieces of Vepar scattered across the end of the pier. When he was done, he stood and admired his work, huffing and puffing. Kathy could see blood sprayed across his face in the moonlight. The sword in his hand disappeared, and he reached down to help lift Kathy back onto the dock.

He looked at her and said, "Grab the other end of the net over there and help me round up the body before anyone sees."

FIND ALL THE BOOKS IN THE COVEN SERIES!

More by the Author

To find more books by the author, visit
DavidNethBooks.com/Books

* * *

Subscribe to his newsletter to be the first to know of new
releases and special deals!
DavidNethBooks.com/Newsletter

* * *

**If you enjoyed the book, please consider leaving a
review on Goodreads or the retailer you bought it from.**
Reviews help potential readers determine whether
they'll enjoy a book, so any comments on what you
thought of the story would be very helpful!

About the Author

David Neth is the author of the Coven series, the Under the Moon series, Heat series, the Fuse series, and other stories. He lives in Batavia, NY, where he dreams of a successful publishing career and opening his own bookstore.

Also writes small town romance as D. Allen.

www.DavidNethBooks.com

www.facebook.com/DavidNethBooks